Dedication

To my family for their endless support.

The St. Valentine's Situation

A Pinewood Corners Sweet Romance

CAROL BABINEAUX

THE ST. VALENTINE'S SITUATION
A Pinewood Corners Sweet Romance

Copyright © 2024. Carol Babineaux

All rights reserved. No part of this publication may be reproduced, distributed, or transmitted in any form or by any means, including photocopying, recording, or other electronic or mechanical methods, without the prior written permission of the copyright holder, except in the case of brief quotations embodied in critical reviews and certain other noncommercial uses permitted by copyright law.

Book Design by
Transcendent Publishing
www.transcendentpublishing.com

Edited by Lori Lynn

ISBN: 979-8-9896548-8-8

This book is a work of fiction. Names, characters, and incidents are a product of the author's imagination or used fictitiously. Any resemblance to persons, living or dead, is entirely coincidental.

Printed in the United States of America.

Chapter One

My heart leapt into my throat and my body went numb when I saw the silhouette outlined against the building in the darkness of the late January morning.

Was that a man prowling near the front windows of the library?

I glanced around and saw no other cars in the lot. Where had he come from? I shut off my headlights and reached for my cell phone to dial the sheriff's office.

Mindy Cranston, one of the part-time dispatchers, picked up the line.

"Wingate County sheriff's office, this is Mindy," she chirped.

"Hey, Mindy," I replied. "It's Lacey. I'm in the parking lot at the library, and there's a strange man lurking around the building. Can you send someone to check it out?"

"Strange man?" Mindy asked. "Is he cute?"

I squeezed my eyes shut in frustration. Mindy had always been a flighty sort of girl. "Mindy, it's still dark. I have no idea what he looks like. Nor do I have any idea who he is or what his intentions are. I just pulled in to open the library, and there's a man creeping around outside peeping in the windows. Can you send someone? Is Tom on shift this morning?" Tom Willis was a friend who briefly dated my best friend Mikki in high school and had recently returned to accept the role of Wingate County's Deputy Sheriff.

"I'll send Sheriff Weaver over," she replied, clicking off the line abruptly. I felt fidgety and impatient just sitting in the parking lot. Maybe I should drive off, for safety's sake. But as the head librarian, I felt it was my duty to be here when the sheriff arrived. My car was still running, and the heater was suddenly too warm. I reached down to adjust the temperature so I wouldn't end up cooking myself to death in the parking lot. When I looked back up, the suspicious looking man was gone.

Where did he go? I knew that I should stay in the safety of my car, but an intense curiosity and concern for the library spurred me to action. After all, Sheriff Weaver was on his way, and the county municipal building was within walking distance. I thought of the self-defense course I recently took at the community center. *I can take care of myself.*

Steeling my nerves, I grabbed my purse and slung the strap over my head so it hung cross-body. I threaded my keys through my fingers so that the points stuck out between my knuckles. This guy would get a face full of metal if he tried to mess with me.

I opened the door as quietly as I could and slipped out into the bracing chill of the dark morning. The sun was rising, albeit behind a heavy cloud cover that left the atmosphere gray and dim.

Crouching beside the car, I leaned my back into the door and gently pushed it shut. I duck-walked around the car in a squat, keeping my head below the height of the car windows. I stopped behind the front panel of the passenger side and peered over the car's hood, holding my breath as I gazed towards the building, looking for the mysterious stranger.

"Are you the librarian?" A clear masculine voice rang from behind me. Startled, I gasped and fell backwards out of my squat and felt the icy pavement come up hard under my backside. I brandished my key-fist as I speed crawled backwards like a deranged crab.

"Get back! I've called the police! Who are you?" I struggled to scramble to my feet without taking my eyes off the man.

He stood behind my car, off to the side, in a relaxed posture with his hands stuffed casually into the pockets of his puffy olive green coat. A battered leather messenger bag was slung over the coat by a strap that extended diagonally over his chest.

"Martin. Martin Weaver. That was a thrilling performance, by the way. I especially liked how you managed to move all the way around the car while staying in a crouch. Very talented. You must work out."

"Excuse me," I sputtered, no longer frightened and well on my way to being angry. "I pull into the parking lot, ready to start a normal day, and see some suspicious character lurking around the front of the building, peeping in the windows! What was I supposed to think?"

"It's not exactly the middle of the night, and this isn't a residence, it's a public building," he pointed out in a calm, rational voice. "I wanted to get started on research for a project. I thought it best to get here as soon as the library opened." He kept his hands in his pockets as he lifted his shoulders.

Somewhat mollified, I lowered my keys. "The library opens at 7:30."

"So the sign says. I was hoping someone was inside already and might let me in a few minutes early," he said.

I looked more closely at him in the dim pre-dawn light. He looked to be in his early thirties, tall, with a slender build. I couldn't see much of him because he was wearing a beanie pulled low. Between his beard and his scarf, his face was merely a nose and eyes.

Headlights turned into the parking lot and Sheriff Weaver's patrol car pulled up next to mine. I instantly recognized the tall and slim older man with silver brush cut hair. As he got out of the car wearing his standard khaki uniform, he approached the younger man. To my surprise, Sheriff Weaver threw his arms enthusiastically around the stranger and greeted him warmly.

"Martin! When did you get to town?"

"Late last night," the man replied, clapping the sheriff on the back. "I didn't want to wake you. I was going to call you later this morning."

The sheriff turned to me with a wide smile. "Lacey, this is my youngest son, Martin," he gestured proudly at the man beside him. "Martin, meet Lacey Crawford, head librarian of the Pinewood Corners Public Library."

Weaver. He said his name was Martin Weaver. I should have known. I felt my face redden as I realized that I had just called the sheriff to report that his son was a potential intruder.

"Nice to meet you," I said. "Sorry about the panicked call to the police. I wasn't expecting anyone to be prowling around the library this time of the morning, and I know all my regular patrons, and … " I trailed off, feeling foolish.

"Nonsense, you did the right thing. You can't be too careful these days," Sheriff Weaver assured me. "I don't know why Martin felt that he had to sneak over here under cover of darkness, anyway." The older man chuckled and elbowed his son in the ribs.

"Well, let's go ahead and get those doors unlocked," I said with forced cheer as I strode towards the library. The men trailed behind me, and I could hear them talking about Sheriff Weaver's upcoming wedding. He was marrying Mikki's grandmother on Valentine's Day. I realized that the son had likely come to town for his father's wedding.

I unlocked the main door of the library and entered, punching in the alarm code and switching on the lights. The two men were still talking just inside the doors as I continued heading deeper into the building, flipping on more lights and booting up computers. I stopped in my office to deposit my purse and my lunch. I removed my coat, scarf, and hat.

Turning to the small mirror next to the door, I studied my reflection. The freckles across my nose stood out on my winter-pale face and a dusting of plum eyeshadow and a light coating of mascara complimented my wide green eyes. I smoothed my slightly frizzy auburn hair, then rooted around in my bag for my lipstick. I slicked some mauve color over my pallid lips. Satisfied with my appearance for the moment, I headed back to the main floor. The man … *Martin*, I reminded myself, was leaning on the checkout desk. Sheriff Weaver was nowhere to be seen, and I assumed he had gone back to the station.

"Nice little library you have here," Martin said, casting his gaze around as I approached. I had worked hard to make the library a clean, well-stocked and modern facility in the five years since I had become the head librarian.

"Thank you, I'm rather proud of it," I said. "You mentioned a project. What exactly are you looking for?"

"Do you house historical records here, or do I need to find the historical society?" He had removed his beanie and scarf, and in the lights over the main desk, I could see that his hair was wavy and on the longish side, tumbling over his forehead and the tops of his ears. His locks were dark brown with deep auburn highlights that matched the ginger tone of his mustache and beard, which were neatly trimmed in contrast to his hair. He had thick, straight eyebrows and thin, yet shapely lips under his mustache.

My heart quickened its pace as I studied his slim form in well-worn jeans that molded to his exceptional physique. I had not looked at a man that way—or felt that tingle of attraction— since my divorce. This realization caused my heart to beat faster with apprehension instead of lust. I realized that Martin was still standing there, waiting for my answer, and things were getting awkward. *Get it together, Lacey!* I gave my head a slight shake.

"Uh … yes, we have all the town's historical records here, in the reference room. It was a bit of a struggle with the ladies from the Pinewood Corners Historical Society to get the records, but the library has far better facilities for security, organization, storage, and climate control. You'll have to read everything on site, as we don't allow them to be removed from the library. Some records have to be requested, and you'll need to wear gloves to handle them."

"Of course," he replied in a tone that implied that it would be scandalous to do otherwise. "I'm familiar with how to handle antique documents." As proof, he extracted a pair of white cotton gloves from his pocket and waved them in the air.

I raised my eyebrows. "Okay, then. I'll get the reference room unlocked for you. You'll need to sign in and out when you're using the room." I led the way towards the back of the library and Martin followed.

"You're pretty serious about security around here," he observed as he watched me punch in the code to unlock the door to the reference room.

"I instituted new security measures after some documents went missing a few years back," I said. "These papers and diaries and ledgers may seem like merely old dusty books to some people, but they're living pieces of the history of this town. They can't be replaced."

Martin didn't reply. He just gave me a long, speculative look. He signed in on the tablet by the door and placed his worn leather messenger bag on one of the tables and began removing his coat.

"Staying a while, then?" I asked him. "What exactly can I help you find?"

"I'm researching for a book on lost treasures of America. I'm looking for information on the missing necklace of Maeve McKenna."

My eyes widened. "Really? That's fascinating, but it will probably be a short chapter in your book. Maeve McKenna disappeared along with the necklace back in 1865, and no one has been able to find a trace of either one since."

"I've heard the legends," he said. "I spent most of my summers in Pinewood Corners, visiting my dad." At my inquiring look, he said, "My parents divorced when I was six. Mom moved my brother and sister and me a couple of counties over. I was always intrigued by the legend of the town's founding family. What imaginative boy wouldn't be? Arranged marriage, wealthy patriarch, missing bride, missing jewelry. Did she abscond with the necklace? Was she kidnapped? It's a fascinating tale."

"Well, some records are on microfiche, some have been converted to digital, and most are boxed up." I gestured to the rows of sliding shelves behind Martin. "They're organized by year, so it should be easy for you to find the materials relevant to your search."

"Thank you," he said, pulling a laptop, legal pad, journal, and pens and highlighters from his bag. As I watched his long and narrow hands arrange his supplies, I noticed that his left hand was bare. *It doesn't matter,* I told myself, shoving the observation from my mind. *Keep it strictly business.*

"If you come across anything that's restricted, just press this button," I said, pointing to a buzzer on the wall next to the door. "I or one of the assistant librarians will be in to help you."

"Thank you," he repeated, not looking up as he booted up his laptop. I felt firmly dismissed as I stepped out, closing the door softly behind me.

*   *   *

I pushed my bangs out of my eyes and glanced at the big clock on the wall over the checkout desk. It was nearly time to close up the library for the day. It had been a long and crazy day, filled with rambunctious children and lots of patrons seeking various books and materials. I saw Miriam O'Connell, one of my part-time volunteers, approaching the desk. She slid the now-empty book cart into place next to the others that were lined up beside the checkout counter.

"That's everything," she said with a satisfied air, brushing her hands together. Her chunky silver rings clanked.

"Thanks, Miriam," I said, smiling warmly at her. "You can go ahead and take off if you'd like. I can finish closing up."

Miriam grinned and shook her head, her long silver braids trailing over her shoulders. "No can do, boss. There are still a few patrons in here and I wouldn't feel right leaving you here all alone. Especially after the incident with the *prowler* this morning." Her blue eyes sparkled as she winked.

I laughed. "Behave, before I fire you," I joked.

"Nice fella," she said as she pulled the spray bottle of cleaner and a roll of paper towels out from under the counter and began to spray down the surface.

"Who's a nice fella?" I asked.

"The prowler, of course," she replied without looking up from her wipe down. "He buzzed a couple of times from the reference room, and I helped him find some things. Seems real intelligent and polite. No wedding ring, either."

"Oh. I hadn't noticed," I replied. *Liar!* my inner voice shouted. *You definitely noticed that he wasn't wearing a ring!* "When did he leave?" I tried to sound casual.

"He didn't."

"You're kidding." I glanced back towards the reference room and saw that the lights were indeed still on. The man had been in there all day. I thanked Miriam and headed towards the reference room. I peeked through the narrow window to the side of the door.

Martin was sitting at the table, surrounded by various boxes and stacks of books and papers. An old leather-bound ledger was open in front of him and he was studying it intently and taking notes on a legal pad. His hair was raised in a tangled nest of waves, as if he had been running his hands through the auburn locks. A pair of wire-framed glasses perched low on the bridge of his nose.

I reached up and tapped gently on the door. Martin glanced up from the ledger as I pushed the door open.

"Hi, I didn't realize you were still working. We're about to close up for the day," I said.

Martin ran his hand through his hair, pushing it even higher. He removed his glasses and rubbed his eyes. Blinking, he reached over and picked up his phone, glancing at the screen.

"Wow, I didn't realize it was so late." His gaze traveled over the boxes and stacks of papers all around him. "I guess I'd better clean this up, then."

I shook my head. "That's okay, I can take care of it tomorrow."

"If it's all the same, I'll be back tomorrow, so maybe we can leave it out? Then I can pick up where I left off."

"Sure, that's fine with me," I assured him. I couldn't resist adding, "As long as you promise not to scare the daylights out of me tomorrow morning."

"It's a deal," he replied. He stood and began gathering his things, stuffing the legal pad and pens into his brown messenger bag. I bent to pick up a crumpled piece of yellow paper from the floor. Smoothing it out, I saw that it was covered with cramped writing, most of which looked like some sort of shorthand. Martin looked up, saw the paper, and snatched it from my hand.

"Old notes." He jammed the paper into his bag. "I'm going in a different direction."

I plastered what I hoped was an understanding smile on my face as I waited for him to finish collecting his things.

"Did you find what you were looking for?" I asked, unable to contain my curiosity any longer.

Martin eyed me warily as he buckled the straps of his carryall. "I think I may have found some interesting leads. But I may need to arrange to speak to some people around town."

Martin finally shrugged into his olive green coat and tugged on his beanie and scarf. I stood back and let him pass through the doorway and then I closed the door behind us and punched in the code to lock the door. Martin waved his hand in an "after you" gesture, and I led the way back towards the front desk. Miriam was still there, waiting for us, her hands in the pockets of her faded denim overalls.

"All the other patrons are checked out, and they've gone," she said and turned to Martin. "Find what you were looking for?" she asked, echoing my earlier question.

"I think so, I found some great leads," he said with a nod, "but I have a lot more to do while I'm in town."

Miriam grinned, and her gaze traveled from me to Martin. "So you'll be around for a little while, then?" she asked.

"Yes," he replied, "I'll be here through Valentine's Day for my dad's wedding. I hope that will be enough time to complete my research."

A loud gurgling sound erupted from the region of Martin's stomach. A blush trailed up his face all the way to his hairline. He shuffled his feet. "Excuse me. I guess I forgot to eat lunch."

"Where are you staying?" Miriam asked him.

"A place called the PC B&B. I suppose it means Pinewood Corners Bed-and-Breakfast." His tone indicated that he did not approve of cute abbreviations.

It occurred to me that I had not seen a car in the parking lot this morning when I had discovered Martin lurking outside. He had been at the library all day. I was tired from the busy shift, but I was also on fire with curiosity about what

Martin might have discovered about the town's most famous legend. Against my better judgment, I decided to try to dig for more information.

"I can drop you off there, if you'd like," I offered. My three-year-old daughter, Claire, was with my ex-husband, Jed, so I was free for the evening.

Martin inclined his head towards me. "I would be grateful," he said formally.

"I'm curious. Didn't you rent a car?"

"I tried." He adjusted the strap of his bag. "The rental agencies around here were all out of cars, what with the festival crowds arriving in town. I was lucky to get a room at the B&B because of a last-minute cancellation."

The three of us trooped out the front doors together. Martin and Miriam exchanged goodbyes as Miriam headed towards her rusty pickup, and I locked up and punched in the alarm code.

"Well, let's hit the road," I said cheerfully and walked towards my blue sedan. Martin followed, and I saw his eyes travel to the car seat strapped in the back.

"I have a daughter, Claire. She's almost four," I said, answering the question he hadn't asked.

"You're married?" Martin asked. Call me crazy, but I thought I detected the barest hint of disappointment in his voice.

"I was," I replied. "High school sweethearts. We divorced almost two years ago now."

Martin grunted in reply and settled back against the cloth seat as I put the car in gear and we pulled out of the parking lot and onto the road. Another loud stomach gurgle pierced the silence.

"Here," I said, reaching into the center console and tossing a small bag of goldfish crackers his way. "Perks of having a toddler. You always have snacks handy."

He ripped the small bag open and popped a handful of crackers into his mouth. I winced at the sound of chewing and reached out to turn on the radio. The bluetooth automatically picked up the music app on my phone, which was set to my favorite playlist. I had titled it *Legendary Ladies* because it featured my favorite female artists such as Stevie Nicks, Taylor Swift, and Lady Gaga. I loved making and naming playlists. "Edge of Seventeen" came blaring out of the car's speakers, and I couldn't resist singing along with the chorus.

"Ooh, baby, ooh, said ooooh!" I crooned along with Stevie, tapping the steering wheel to the beat. I glanced over at Martin. He looked visibly pained. I grinned.

"What's wrong? You don't enjoy a little Stevie Nicks?" I hit the skip button on my steering wheel and the track switched to "Bad Romance" by Lady Gaga.

Martin's face morphed from annoyance to abject horror.

I laughed and asked him, "Fine, what music do you like?"

"As far as I'm concerned, most music is frivolous. I prefer music without lyrics, classical or jazz."

We rolled up to a red light and I pulled my phone from my purse. I opened the music app and searched for a premade classical playlist and popped it on. It wasn't my *Legendary Ladies*, but it was tolerable and rather soothing.

Martin took a deep breath and leaned his head back against the headrest, closing his eyes with a sigh as a violin played. I noticed that he was now clutching an empty cracker bag in one hand.

"So, do you have bigger plans for dinner than a handful of crackers?" I asked him, knowing that the B&B didn't serve an evening meal.

His eyes popped open. "I have some protein bars in my suitcase at the B&B."

"That's not proper sustenance," I scoffed. "Would you like to swing by a drive-through and pick something up? Or we could stop by the El."

Martin's head snapped up. "The El?" he asked. "Is that place still around?"

"You bet, it's practically an institution in this town," I replied.

The El, short for the El Royale, was a classic diner complete with 1960s space-age glitter formica and vinyl and a jukebox that played nothing but 80s music. It was a quirky slice of the past, and they served quintessential dishes like meatloaf platters, chicken fried steak, patty melts, and, in my opinion, the best fried pickles in the entire county.

"Is old man Crowder still there?" Martin asked, referring to the original owner.

"Nope, a woman named Darlene Meyer bought the place a few years ago. She's quite a pistol, and she's kept the El running like Swiss clockwork." I pulled to a stop sign and shot a look at my passenger.

Martin had a faraway look on his face. "My dad used to take me and my brother and sister down to the El for dinner on Saturday nights when we visited him as kids. I always got a grilled cheese sandwich and a side of fried pickles." His dreamy smile convinced me. I popped on my turn signal.

"Enough said. We're going to the El." I turned the wheel and headed up Oak Boulevard towards the diner.

Chapter Two

The parking lot was almost full when we pulled in. The diner was a popular spot in town with both the locals and the tourists. I pulled into a vacant space and turned the engine off. Martin popped his door open immediately and jumped out.

As I was getting my things together, I was surprised by the driver's side door being yanked open. I glanced up, startled. Martin was standing there, holding the door open with one hand, and holding out his other hand towards me, palm up. I blushed, feeling awkward. The only man I had ever dated was my ex-husband Jed, and Jed had never once opened a car door for me. I had no idea how to react. I fell back on my comfort zone, which was sarcasm.

"This isn't a date, Sir Galahad," I informed him. Instead of being offended, he leaned into the game.

With a deep bow and a decent British accent, he said, "As the son of Sir Lancelot, and the most pure and perfect of knights, I beseech thee, dear lady, to take my hand and I shall guide thee to sustenance."

"You are a complete twit," I said with a barely straight face as I swatted his hand away. I pulled myself out of the car and shut the door. "Come on, o knight so pure." I couldn't help but smile then as he straightened up and followed behind me, head held high, still imitating Sir Galahad.

I shook my head ruefully as we made our way to the glass doors of the restaurant. Martin reached around me and pulled the handle, opening the door and gesturing for me to enter. Warm air carrying the delicious smells of frying meat and fresh yeast rolls beckoned us inside. The distinct synthesizer tones of "Jump" by Van Halen punctuated the buzz of lively conversation. The diner was busy, as usual, and I glanced around, hoping that we could still get a table.

A curvy older woman with platinum hair done up in a tall twist came towards us with a broad smile on her candy-pink lips, her bright plastic pink earrings swinging. "Hey, Lacey! Who's your new friend?" she asked.

"Hi, Darlene. This is Martin Weaver. Sheriff Weaver's son." I gestured towards Martin. "Martin, this is Darlene Meyer, the new owner of the El."

"Hi," Martin said, "pleased to meet you. I love this place. We used to come here as kids."

"Sounds about right," Darlene said. "I'll bet you were a little cutie, too, just like your handsome daddy." Martin blushed and Darlene laughed, a deep and raspy chuckle.

"Well, I'm all out of tables right now, hon, so you kids can sit at the back counter, or if you don't mind, you can share a table with another couple. I'm sure your best friend won't mind." Darlene nodded towards the front corner.

"Mikki's here?" I asked.

"Right over there. She's having dinner with her main squeeze."

I followed her gaze and saw that a petite and pretty brunette was seated in a booth across from a stunningly gorgeous blond man. As if she could feel our eyes on her, Michaela Branson turned and looked at us. A smile broke out on her face as she recognized me. She leaned forward and said something to her date before she jumped up and came towards us.

"Lacey, hi!" she said, giving me a brief hug. "And who might this be?"

"This is Martin. He's doing some research at the library, and he's here for the wedding. Are you sure you don't mind if we join you?"

"Of course we don't mind," she said to me. Looking at Martin, she said, "Please join us. I'm sure Michael won't mind at all."

Clutching my elbow, she steered me towards the booth and whispered, "Is this the infamous prowler from this morning that I heard about?"

I shot her a quizzical look.

"I ran into Mindy Cranston at the Fresh Stop this afternoon," she explained. I sighed internally. This prowler story would be all over town by morning.

"He was—I mean, he is, but he's not."

Mikki's brows drew together in confusion.

"Never mind," I said in exasperation.

Mikki slid into the booth next to Michael. "Scoot over, babe," she said. "Lacey and her friend Martin are joining us."

"Sure," her boyfriend said, scooting himself closer to the wall. "Lacey," he acknowledged me and held out a hand across the table to Martin. "I'm Michael Brandon," he introduced himself.

Martin leaned forward and grasped his hand in a quick shake. "Martin Weaver," he said.

"Any relation to Sheriff Weaver?" Michael asked. Martin slid across the teal blue vinyl next to me, careful to keep plenty of distance between us.

"I'm his youngest son," Martin confirmed.

"Oh, I remember you!" Mikki exclaimed. "Your dad used to bring you in here on Saturday nights back in the day. I used to come here with my Grandma Jo on Saturday nights, too."

"Yes, we all loved coming here. Do they still make good grilled cheese?" Martin asked, hope in his voice.

"The best," Mikki smiled broadly. "I love it with tomato and bacon."

I picked up a menu from the holder in the center of the table, grimacing at the film of sticky grease on the plastic coating. I glanced at it briefly and offered it to Martin. He shook his head.

"So," Michael said, draping his arm around Mikki's shoulders, "I guess you're in town for the wedding? And the Sweetheart Soiree festival?"

"The wedding, sure, and I'm also working on a project. A book on the lost treasures of America."

Mikki snapped her fingers and pointed at Martin. "The necklace!" she cried. "Maeve McKenna's lost necklace."

Having grown up in Pinewood Corners, I was well-acquainted with the legend of the town's founder, Merrick McKenna. An orphan, McKenna had sailed to America from Ireland as a lad of fourteen and had made his fortune with trapping. He eventually settled in the area, purchased land, and built a mercantile and a boarding house from the wood of the pines that were plentiful in the area and named the newly minted town Pinewood Corners.

As he built his fortune over the years, the only thing missing from his life was a family. He sent word to his homeland seeking a bride, and six months later, he returned to town with 18-year-old Maeve in tow. The stories all told that she was shy and sweet, a petite and lovely tender blonde who missed Ireland dearly.

The couple settled into married life, and two sons arrived in quick succession. The stories told that Maeve found a measure of happiness raising her small sons, but was still melancholy and homesick much of the time. At her husband's urging, she had organized the town's very first festival, Lights by the Lake. The holiday festival was a hit, and Maeve found much fulfillment from planning and executing the event. So much so, in fact, that she immediately began planning for a Valentine's Day festival, and Pinewood Corners was reborn as a "festival town."

However, shortly before the first Valentine's festival, people noticed that Maeve was once again appearing melancholy, and she had begun isolating herself. There were also rumors of an unidentified "gentleman caller" spotted skulking in the side yard of McKenna Manor. Merrick McKenna did his best to cheer his wife up, and he commissioned a one-of-a-kind 15-carat, heart-shaped, cushion cut ruby pendant, fully encased by diamond chips, hanging from a delicate platinum chain, as a Valentine's gift for his beloved bride. Two days before the festival was to launch, however, McKenna reported that Maeve was missing, along with the priceless necklace.

Gossip and rumors abounded. Had Maeve been taken against her will, stolen along with the necklace? Did she steal the necklace and use the money to return to her homeland? Did she run off with the unidentified man seen around her home in the prior days? Despite all of the gossip and speculation, the festival went on as planned, and neither Maeve nor the necklace ever turned up. Merrick McKenna never married again. He hired housekeepers and nannies to help and raise his sons, and by all accounts, died a rich, bitter, and lonely old man.

Shaking myself out of the past, I came back to the present.

"Yes, actually," Martin was saying. "That's how I ran into Lacey. I spent the day at the library doing research." The couple smiled in response.

"Mikki and Michael are opening a bakery in town," I told Martin.

"Really? That's great. When are you opening?

"Next week is the grand opening," Michael replied, giving Mikki's shoulders an affectionate squeeze.

"You may have seen Michael and Mikki on TV. The Culinary Channel did a live special covering the cookie bake off during the Lights by the Lake holiday festival over Christmas," I informed Martin. His eyebrows went up. I realized that his eyes were an unusual shade of clear light brown, almost amber, with lighter flecks that appeared golden. I felt that tingle of attraction again, traveling up my core like electricity.

"I don't really watch television," he said, "other than news or an occasional documentary."

We were interrupted by the arrival of Darlene, with her order pad.

"Hi, kids, have we decided?" She raised one thinly penciled eyebrow at Martin and me.

"I'll have the club sandwich and a side of fried pickles," I told her.

"A grilled cheese sandwich, on sourdough, and some fried pickles, please," Martin said. Popping her gum, Darlene scribbled the orders on her pad.

"How about some Coke floats?" she asked. Martin's eyes lit up.

"I'd like that!" he said.

"Just a plain old Diet Coke for me, please," I said.

"Okay, I'll make sure all your meals come out together." With a wink, Darlene sashayed away from our table.

Mikki laughed. "It's a good thing my Grandma Jo locked down your dad," she told Martin, "because I think Darlene is in the market for her next husband."

"I don't know Mrs. Morton too well," he said, referring to Mikki's grandmother, "but my dad sure seems happy."

"Oh, I guess you and I will soon be related by marriage," Mikki said, her hazel eyes wide.

Martin agreed and took a sip of his water.

Michael asked, "So, Martin, how's your research going?"

"It's going well. I may have uncovered some interesting elements to the story. Are you all natives of Pinewood Corners?" he asked.

We all shook our heads.

"I just arrived in town last year to help out my mom after she became ill," Michael explained. He gestured to his sweetheart beside him. "Mikki grew up here off and on. She traveled with her parents and their theater troupe a lot."

"I did grow up here," I said, "but I didn't move here until the second grade. That was when I came to live with my aunt."

Martin looked at me quizzically, but he didn't press for details. I was glad for it, because I didn't want to get into the whole story of my archeologist parents and how they disappeared in the Yucatan Mountains when I was eight.

"And that's when we met, and became best friends," Mikki chimed in.

"Why do you ask?" I inquired.

"I found some records that link to a Mary Elizabeth O'Grady who worked for a prominent family in Pinewood Corners at the time the necklace and the bride went missing. I would love to know if the family still has any descendants in the area. They may have family paperwork or records that could help me out," Martin replied.

"Why don't you have your dad ask around? He's lived here all his life," Mikki chimed in.

Martin shook his head. "I think his capacity as sheriff is intimidating. I wouldn't want people thinking the law was involved in any way."

"Then you should ask my Grandma Jo," Mikki said. "She's lived here all her life, and she knows everybody."

"I might take you up on that," Martin replied. Just then, Darlene returned bearing a large tray loaded with plates and glasses.

We all moved our water glasses and silverware aside and leaned back to make room for her to set our food down. Conversation ceased temporarily as we all dug in.

Eventually, we had nothing but scraps left on our plates, and everyone settled in, full and satisfied.

"Lacey, I have to use the ladies' room," Mikki said.

"Okay," I replied, too full and lazy to get up. Mikki looked miffed.

"Come with me," she pleaded.

"Oh, fine," I groused. I waved my hands in a shooing gesture at Martin. "Excuse me, while I'm forced to escort my best friend to the restroom." Martin moved, and I slid out of the booth. I noticed that he didn't offer his hand this time.

Mikki had barely pushed into the door of the ladies' room when she pounced.

"He's kind of cute, what's the story?" She set a huge brown leather purse on the counter and began digging around in its depths.

"Story? There isn't any story. I met him just this morning. He's a patron at the library, he's in town for his dad's wedding, and he was hungry. I was giving him a ride to the PC B&B, and we decided to grab some dinner. As friends. Because it was dinnertime." I crossed my arms over my chest. "And that's it," I said firmly.

Mikki looked disappointed. "Do you think he's handsome?" she asked. She triumphantly pulled a tube of lip gloss from her purse and began applying it.

"I don't know, maybe," I said. "It's hard to tell under all that hair. I don't even know him. He seems distant and scholarly one minute, and the next, he's acting like a goofball." I turned on one of the faucets and sudsed up my hands. "I'll tell you one thing, he does *not* like my music."

She laughed. "No Stevie Nicks, huh?" she teased. "Uh-oh, that may be a deal breaker."

"Anyway, he's only here for a few weeks, then he'll go back to wherever he came from, so there's no point even speculating about this," I said firmly.

"But that could be perfect for you," Mikki insisted. "Cupid's Ball is in a couple of weeks. You could at least get your feet wet. You've never dated anyone but Jed. You need to stick your neck out a little."

"You're mixing your metaphors," I said.

"Nerd," she teased.

"Geek," I shot back, and we collapsed into giggles, just like we used to do when we were kids.

When we strolled back to the table, Martin and Michael were deep in discussion about the Maeve McKenna legend. Apparently, Michael was unfamiliar with the tale, and Martin was more than happy to regale him with the story.

"So no one ever found any trace of her?" Michael asked, leaning forward with his mouth agape and his pale blue eyes wide.

"No, not a thing," Martin said, slapping his palm on the formica table. "No Maeve, no necklace. And the odd thing is that McKenna never even had the chance to give his wife the necklace. He had a grand plan to present it to her at the inaugural Cupid's Ball on Valentine's Day, but Maeve disappeared on February 12th that year, the same day that Merrick discovered the necklace was gone from the safe in his home. No one other than Merrick McKenna and the jewelry designer even saw the necklace before it went missing. A few concept sketches have survived. If it exists, that necklace could be worth upwards of eight million today."

Martin's eyes were large, and he practically glowed with passion for his subject matter. The man seemed to be a real history buff. His enthusiasm for the subject changed his features from average to quite handsome.

Michael leaned against the booth and let out a long, low whistle. "That's a pretty penny," he said.

"Indeed," Martin replied.

"Would the money belong to you, if you were to find it?" Mikki asked.

"Actually, if the McKenna family has any living descendants, the necklace would technically belong to them," Martin said.

"I think the family line died out in the 1980s," I said.

Darlene reappeared with the check. Martin leaned forward and extracted his wallet.

"I've got this," he said, tossing a credit card onto the tray with the check. I snatched the card up.

"Oh no you don't," I said. I glanced down at the card. "Martin P. Weaver, huh? What does the 'P' stand for?"

"None of your business," Martin said, grabbing the card and putting it back on the tray. After some verbal wrangling, and repeated insistence from Martin, we all finally agreed to allow him to cover the bill.

*   *   *

We parted with Mikki and Michael in the parking lot. I watched the couple climb into Michael's shiny black pickup and drive away as Martin and I strolled to my sedan. I hit the button to unlock the doors and Martin went directly to the passenger door and opened it.

As he climbed in, I wondered if I had offended him more than he had let on when I had refused his helping hand earlier. I was vaguely disappointed that I seemed to have screwed up having him offer to open the car door for me, and I had no idea why I felt that way. Shaking it off, I settled myself in the driver's seat and started the car.

Classical music filled the interior of the car as I pulled out onto the cold, dark street and headed towards the B&B.

I squinted, annoyed, as the vehicle behind me closed in and the headlights glared into my eyes in the rearview mirror. I accelerated, putting more distance between the vehicles. The small, low-slung white car then pulled into the left lane and roared past us.

The car looked familiar to me because it was just like the one that Jed had bought right after we graduated college, a white Dodge Avenger. Jed had loved that silly car, babying it and washing it every weekend. He had treasured it and only parted with it when we needed to upgrade to a larger vehicle when I became pregnant with Claire.

Martin was quiet as I drove, but the silence between us didn't feel as awkward.

"Tomorrow is Wednesday," I blurted out.

"Thanks for the news bulletin," Martin replied in a dry tone.

"Funny, very funny. I mean that the library doesn't open until nine on Wednesdays."

"Nine!" Martin cried out, sounding anguished. "I have a lot more research to conduct. Is there any way that I can get in earlier?"

"No, sorry. I have to pick up my daughter in the morning and get her to preschool."

Martin flopped back against the seat and sighed. "Well, at least that gives me a chance to have breakfast with my dad and catch up. I'm sure he'll want to have dinner with me and my brother and sister when they arrive in town next week. Then I can spend part of the morning transcribing some of my notes," he muttered.

"There you go, there's always a bright side," I said, pulling up to the curb in front of the B&B. "Do you have a ride tomorrow?" I asked him.

"I'll figure something out," he replied, fishing in the back seat for his messenger bag.

"Okay, good night, then. Thanks for dinner."

Martin leaned down into the car to peer at me. "Thanks for the ride—and the goldfish," he said, before shutting the passenger door and strolling off towards the front door of the B&B.

I watched him walk away, and I admitted to myself that he actually might be kind of cute, after all. I switched the music to my favorite playlist and headed for home, singing along with Taylor Swift at the top of my lungs.

*   *   *

I unlocked the door of my little cottage and stepped inside. Decorated in bright colors and opulent fabrics in the bohemian style, this place was my personal sanctuary. I absolutely loved it.

My two dogs, Jethro and Elly May, came rushing at me with snuffles and wags. My ex, Jed, was constantly teased about his name because of Jed Clampett on the old show *The Beverly Hillbillies* and he thought it would be hilarious to name our dogs after two other characters on the show. We named our big, clumsy black lab mix Jethro and our delicate white chihuahua mix Elly May. I let the dogs out into the yard and went to my room to change my clothes.

Peeling off the layers of my conservative work clothes and dropping them to the floor, I reached for my old fuzzy turquoise bathrobe and my hot pink slipper socks. I went to the bathroom and turned on the light. After removing a Barbie doll from the sink, I turned on the hot water and pulled my hair back into a low bun with a purple velvet scrunchie. The warm water felt wonderful on my face, and the rich foam of my facial cleanser washed the day away. Feeling refreshed, I slathered on some moisturizer and headed to the patio door to let the dogs in.

I settled down with a cup of chamomile tea and breathed in the soothing and delicate apple-like scent of the brew. After flipping around on the various streaming services, I discovered that there wasn't anything that held my interest this evening. I tossed the remote aside and reached for my journal. The house hummed with silence, save the rumble of the refrigerator and the gentle snoring of the dogs.

I had been big on journaling for most of my life, starting after the disappearance of my parents. My aunt had taken me to see a therapist to help me deal with the loss, and the therapist had suggested that I journal my thoughts and feelings so that I was not overwhelmed by them. It had helped me tremendously and the practice had stuck. I opened the pink velour cover and flipped to the next blank page. Clicking the purple gel pen, I jotted down the date and began to write.

How does one "test the waters" of dating? I have never engaged in this popular cultural practice, despite being married, divorced, and the mother of one child. I met Jed in the seventh grade. We started hanging out with mutual friends and one night, in the tenth grade, we were at the movies, and Jed kissed me and asked me to be his girlfriend. Two years after that, he kissed me and asked me to be his wife.

There was no question as to what he was really like, if we would get along, if he was even into me. He was just always "there" in my life— until he wasn't. I was the one who wanted out … when I realized that we were living like roommates. The passion was gone.

Somehow we had allowed it to trickle out, a slow leak that no one noticed until it was too late and the ball had completely deflated. I don't regret letting him go, but I do regret being alone sometimes. Sure, it's nice to watch whatever I want on TV, eat whatever I want for dinner, decorate the house in the style I prefer …

But when there's no one to laugh with you at that TV show and dis- cuss it afterwards, or to admire the new throw pillows you picked out and enjoy them with you, life isn't as much fun. I miss having fun, the kind of fun you have with someone who really gets you and loves you anyway. And yet … I loved my parents dearly, I depended on them, and they disappeared from my life and there was nothing I could do.

Why are these thoughts stirring in my mind, in my soul, now? I've gotten pretty good at pretending I'm okay, that I'm single and loving it. I've almost managed to convince even myself that I love the way I'm living.

What's changed? What's different? Is it all the love-themed stuff around town for the Valentine's festival, all the pink and red glittering hearts and cupids and arrows? The roses everywhere and the library's love poetry contest? Is it the upcoming Cupid's Ball, which has always been about who's going with whom? Is it seeing my best friend so happy and so in love? Seeing her grandmother preparing for her own Valentine's Day wedding? Is it simply because I'm about to turn 30 and I'm taking stock? Is it because the door is firmly closed between me and Jed now that he's dating Elaine Laramie?

I don't know the answers. I only know that I feel very alone in this empty house tonight, and at the same time, I feel frightened to let anyone in. What if all romantic relationships cool off to the point of needing resuscitation? Do they all fade? Jed didn't break my heart, he just neglected it. Tomorrow at least Claire will be back from Jed's and we can pop popcorn and watch a movie together. I must remember to be grateful for the good things in my life, and to not dwell so much on the things that I don't have. But if there is anyone out there written in the stars for me, someone that I can trust to let into my heart, and my life … I really hope that he shows up soon.

I closed the book with a sigh, slid the pen into the elastic loop on the side, and set the journal on the coffee table. Jethro and Elly May followed me into the kitchen, and I gave each of them a dog biscuit after I rinsed out my teacup.

I trailed down the hall toward my bedroom, dogs in tow, and climbed into bed. Propped up on the pillow, trying to relax, I focused on the book in my hands. The lusty maiden was about to rip the doublet off of the sexy pirate, and I realized that the pirate bore a striking resemblance in my mind's eye to Martin Weaver. With a growl of frustration, I tossed the book aside and turned out the light.

Chapter Three

I was running late. After a restless night of tossing and turning, I had overslept and had to skip washing my hair. I roared up to the curb in front of Jed's apartment building, hoping fervently that he had Claire ready to go. I grabbed my phone and hit Jed's number. He picked up on the first ring.

"Hey, we're in the lobby, be right out," Jed said and immediately disconnected the line. *So much for social niceties.* It was just as well, since I didn't really have time to make civil conversation right now. I still had to run Claire to the preschool and get to the library in time to open at nine.

The doors on the front of the building opened and Jed emerged. Tall and thin, wearing khakis and a green polo under a brown jacket, he held Claire's hand. Dressed in her pink coat, jeans, and pink snow boots, she clutched a pink Barbie backpack in her little hand as they headed for my car.

Jed opened the rear passenger side door, lifted Claire up and settled her in the car seat as he handed the backpack to me. The top of his head glowed as his bald spot caught the dome light shining from the roof of the car.

"I thought you'd be here fifteen minutes ago," he said, clicking the final strap in place on the car seat. "I need to get down to the hardware store, we're having our annual pre-spring sale this week."

"Sorry, I woke up late," I responded.

"Trouble sleeping because of the prowler yesterday?" Jed asked. "I heard you caught some creep trying to break into the library."

Yep, the prowler story was all over town this morning.

"No, that was nothing. A misunderstanding," I insisted.

Jed kept his focus on his daughter. He planted a loud, smacking kiss on her forehead.

"Daddy loves you, sugar. I'll see you later. Have a good day!"

Claire pouted. "Why do you have to work today, Daddy? I want you to take me to eat pamcakes for breakfast." She crossed her little arms in front of her chest.

"I'll take you out for *pamcakes* next weekend. Promise."

I watched in the rearview kiddie mirror as he pinky-promised Claire and shut the car door. I sped away from the curb as he waved at both of us, which I always appreciated. I had seen how some of my friends' ex-husbands treated them and counted it a blessing that Jed still treated me more like a distant friend than an unwanted ex-wife. I was the one who had filed for divorce after I realized the passion had drifted away. I didn't exactly feel like it had been a mistake to divorce Jed, and yet during my loneliest moments I did wonder ...

Claire's voice drifted from the backseat. "Mommy, do you have to work today, too?"

"Yes baby, I have to work at the library all day today."

I could hear her muttering about nobody taking her to get "pamcakes," a mispronunciation from the time she was learning to talk that had stuck because now we all referred to pancakes as "pamcakes." I smiled in spite of my harried mood as I turned the car into the parking lot of the preschool.

Little Learners was the only public daycare center in Pinewood Corners. There were several people in town offering home daycare, but I thought Claire would do better in a more structured environment. I lucked out and nabbed the parking spot right next to the front doors.

When I opened the rear door and freed Claire from her car seat, she hopped out with a sunny smile on her face, the pamcake crisis all but forgotten.

"Mommy, will Miss Janelle be here today?" she asked me. Miss Janelle was her favorite teacher at the school. She was a lovely young brunette with enormous blue eyes behind a pair of neon green cat-eye frames with rhinestones glittering in the corners. She seemed to really enjoy working with young children. I liked her.

"I don't know. Let's go in and see!" I grabbed Claire's hand and hitched her backpack over my shoulder as we headed into the building. The bulletin board by the main entrance was decked out with hearts and finger paintings done by the children, all with Valentine themes.

As we walked in, we were greeted by a stout woman with tight gray perm seated behind the front counter.

"Howdy, Crawfords!" she said, her voice as gruff as tires over gravel.

"Hey, Opal," I responded with a wide smile. Opal Gentry looked like a stereotypical truck driver, stout and rough, and the first time I had seen her carrying a box of printer paper like it was Kleenex, I was convinced she was the new delivery driver. I quickly found out that she had been working in early child education for decades when she decided to retire to Pinewood Corners and open a preschool. We were lucky to have her here.

As I signed Claire in, I asked Opal if Janelle was in today.

"Yep, she's in charge of room four," Opal replied, pointing down the hall.

Claire began jumping up and down in excitement, her blonde curly hair bouncing as she sang about how happy she was.

A tall and slender woman with a curtain of dark brown hair that hung straight and thick to her waist stepped out into the hallway. Her bright green frames stood out on her smiling face.

"Do I hear my favorite girl named Claire?" she asked.

With a giggle, Claire skipped towards her. The woman opened the door wider to allow Claire to pass into the room and smiled at me.

"Thanks, Janelle," I told her as I handed off Claire's backpack to her capable hands. "You're looking especially happy this morning."

She blushed prettily and looked at the floor for a moment before meeting my eyes.

"Tom Willis asked me to the Cupid's Ball last night," she said, her voice breathy with controlled excitement. Her deep-set brown eyes shone. Deputy Willis and Mikki had made a brief attempt to rekindle their romance over the holidays, but Mikki only had eyes for Michael. I was happy that Tom had moved on to someone else, but on the other hand, there was yet another budding romance for me to witness.

"Oh, that's wonderful!" I said, ignoring the small pang of jealousy that flared in my chest. "I'd love to hear more about it, but I've got to run."

"I know. Thank you," she replied. "You have a good day, Ms. Crawford." Janelle stepped gracefully back into the classroom and closed the door.

*   *   *

My dash clock read 9:01 when I rolled into the library's parking lot. As I gathered my things and jumped out of the car, I saw that once again Martin Weaver had beaten me to work. He was standing in front of the entrance, looking at his watch. When he looked up and scanned the parking lot, his gaze stopped when he spied me half walking and half running in an undignified trot, my purse and my lunch bag bumping against my hip.

"Sorry," I panted as I approached. "Crazy morning."

Martin merely inclined his head as he stepped aside to allow me to unlock the doors and deactivate the alarm.

As he followed me through the doors, he headed straight for the reference room.

"I'll let you in there in one sec," I said. "Just let me put my stuff down."

Martin raised one hand in acknowledgment as he kept on walking without looking back. I opened my office door, tore off my coat and tossed it on the hook behind the door, and threw my purse and lunch in the cabinet under the mirrored shelf. I paused and glanced in the mirror.

My flame-colored curls were gathered into a messy tumble at the crown of my head, and a few had escaped to trail around the edges of my face. I tried in vain to tuck them into the clip, but I knew it was a losing battle. I slicked on some tinted lip balm and pressed a bit of extra powder underneath my eyes, hoping to hide the dark circles that lingered from my sleepless night. Why I was going the extra mile with my appearance was beyond me. At least, that's what I told myself.

I decided that I looked as good as I was going to get, and went to admit Martin to the reference room. *Heaven forbid he loses another minute of research time,* I thought as I hurried through the stacks towards him.

He was looking at his watch again. It wasn't a smart watch, so he wasn't reading texts. It looked like some sort of fancy analog watch with a bunch of dials and numbers around the rim. I figured the gesture was probably a passive aggressive way to imply that I was causing him an inconvenience. He was wearing the same puffy olive green jacket, with a black sweatshirt and worn jeans underneath today.

"Look, I said I was sorry. It's been a hectic morning, and I got here as quickly as I could," I said defensively as I opened the door.

"No worries, I didn't say anything," Martin replied coolly as he strolled into the room that was still strewn with open boxes and papers from his research efforts the day before. He immediately peeled out of his coat and started dragging his laptop and notes from his leather messenger bag.

I was about to say something else when I heard a loud nasal voice shout from the area of the main checkout desk.

"Yoo hoo! Hello! Is anyone here?"

Oh geez, this is the very last thing I need this morning, I thought as I hustled towards the desk. I would know that nasal tone anywhere. It had to be Rayna Reese, the designated mean girl of Pinewood Corners. Rayna was the only daughter of the town's mayor and she ran the local weekly paper, the *Pinewood Courier,* a paper that her father just happened to own. I braced myself as I rounded the stacks and approached the desk.

Rayna was a strikingly beautiful woman, with lush and shining jet-black hair, a creamy complexion and full rosy lips. Her eyes were a lovely shade of deep violet that contrasted gorgeously with her midnight hair. Unfortunately, her physical beauty was marred by her narcissistic and annoying personality.

I pasted on a pleasant expression. "Rayna, good morning. What brings you down to the library today?" I swallowed hard to keep from coughing as I breathed in the strong floral scent of her perfume.

"Hello, Lacey," Rayna replied, raking her eyes over my simple pencil skirt, scuffed boots and pilled sweater. I stood up straighter, determined that I would not allow her to make me feel inferior.

"What can I do for you?" I asked, hoping that she would come to the point of her visit. I knew for a fact that Rayna had not checked a book out of the library once in the five years that I had been running it.

"I'm here in an official capacity," Rayna replied. She removed a small digital recorder from her designer bag. I was no expert, since I usually bought my purses from the Bargain Boutique, but it looked like a Hermes Birkin bag, or a very good knockoff. "I'm here to interview you for the paper."

"About the poetry contest?" I asked. This year, in conjunction with the town's Sweetheart Soiree festival, I had conceived of a new way to drive traffic to the library's website by launching a love poetry contest. The contestants would submit an original love poem online to the library's website, and the poem voted as the best love poem by the patrons and readers would win a Visa gift card for fifty dollars and have the honor of reading their poem aloud at the opening of the annual Cupid's Ball on Valentine's evening.

Rayna threw back her head and let out a throaty laugh. "No, silly goose. Nobody cares about the poetry contest. I'm here to interview you about the prowler."

Oh good gracious, I thought. Rayna ran the paper like a tabloid and I knew that if I didn't nip this thing in the bud, she would publish a sinister story that would have everyone in town running to Jed's hardware store for deadbolts and pepper spray.

"I'm happy to talk to you off the record," I began, but Rayna shook her head, diamond studs glittering on her earlobes.

"No, I need to record the interview. This is front page material," she insisted.

"It really isn't, Rayna. There was no prowler. It was a misunderstanding. It was merely a patron that I didn't recognize who arrived prior to opening time. It was still dark, and he was just waiting for the doors to be unlocked. Out of an abundance of caution, I called the sheriff before I approached him. Turns out, he's the sheriff's son. He's just doing some research here at the library while he's in town."

Rayna's violet eyes narrowed. "Sheriff Weaver's son? What's he researching that's so important that he felt compelled to arrive at the library before it was even open?" she asked. I could tell she was scenting another story.

"I'm sure I don't have the authority to tell you that."

Rayna clicked a button on the recorder and waved it in my face. "So, Lacey Crawford, Head Librarian of the Pinewood Corners Library, you say that Sheriff Weaver's son was the apparent library lurker, and that he's in town to do important research. Can you tell the readers more about this project?" She extended the recorder.

I just stared at her, my lips pressed together, and shook my head. Reluctantly, Rayna withdrew the recorder and clicked it off.

Just then, the sound of a door opening and shutting heralded the appearance of Martin. He approached the desk and asked, "Do you have any highlighters? Mine have all seemed to decide to dry up at the same time."

"Sure," I said. I wanted to get him out of Rayna's line of sight before she figured out who he was. "I'll bring some to you as soon as I wrap up here."

"Well, hello there," Rayna was trying to be throaty and sexy but she sounded more nasal than ever to my jaded ears. Rayna had made life very difficult for my friend Mikki and me back in high school. I had always gotten off lighter than Mikki because I was dating Jed for half of high school, and Rayna didn't consider tall and gangly Jed worth competing for.

Martin gave her a cursory glance and a brief nod before returning his attention to me.

"Thanks, Lacey," he said, and turned to head down the hall.

"Wait," Rayna called after him. Martin paused and turned around, eyebrows raised.

"Are you the prowler—I mean, the gentleman doing research in town?" she asked, batting her long dark lashes at him.

"I'm here for my dad's wedding," Martin said as he turned and continued down the hall, away from her. She pouted, her shiny red lips protruding like a duck's bill.

"Where is he staying?" she asked me, leaning forward conspiratorially. I shook my head once again.

"I won't violate a patron's privacy," I told her.

"You would do well to remember that the library is a public institution, and your position is determined by the governing leadership of the town," she said, looking up at me slyly as she gathered her recorder and bag.

"Are you threatening me?" I asked incredulously. "Your father may be the mayor, but he can't fire me without cause just because you have some sort of personal issue with me."

Rayna tucked the recorder into her fancy bag and looped it over her forearm.

"You'd be surprised how little grounds are needed to justify firing a municipal employee. There are plenty of people with library degrees that need a job." With that ominous statement, she sauntered off, leaving me open-mouthed and staring after her.

After a moment, I shook myself and went in search of a couple of highlighters for Martin.

I knocked softly on the reference room's door and opened it.

"Here you go," I held out the markers. "Sorry about that. That was—"

"Rayna Reese. I remember her. She was always showing off around town." Martin cut me off and saved me from the need to explain about Rayna. His tone was dismissive, and I got the impression that he wasn't the type of man to fall under the spell of Rayna's dubious charms.

"Right," I said, surprised at the feeling of relief that flooded through me. Martin accepted the markers. Our fingers brushed, and a shiver of electricity shot up my forearm at his touch. I started and yanked my hand away.

Did Martin feel the same sensation? He didn't react in any way, he just turned back to his laptop. I stepped away, intending to leave him to his work.

"Let me know if you need anything else," I said, as Martin looked up at me again.

"What are you doing for lunch?" he asked.

I was caught completely off guard. "Oh, I, um, I usually bring my lunch, so …"

"Well, how about you and I go and grab a sandwich at noon? Is Logan's still around?" he asked, referring to the best sandwich shop in Pinewood Corners.

"It is," I said, pleased that I was being invited to lunch. *Maybe Mikki was right. Maybe it is time for me to get my feet wet, so to speak. Martin's only here for a couple weeks, so it's not a big deal, anyway.*

"I really want someone to bounce my theories off of, and I think a trained librarian would have a logical and organized mind. Even if she does listen to Lady Gaga," Martin elaborated.

I felt my stomach drop with disappointment. He only wanted to take me to lunch to "bounce theories" off of me.

"Hey, Lady Gaga has some very insightful lyrics," I protested.

With an internal sigh, I agreed to go to lunch and talk theories with him. *Looks like my feet are staying bone-dry, after all.* I wasn't certain whether I was relieved or dismayed.

*   *   *

"Agnes, I'm going to grab some lunch, please keep an eye on the checkout desk for the next hour or so," I told my part-time employee. Agnes had been at the library longer than I had. She was a wonderful woman, if a bit flustered at times.

"You'll be in your office if I need you, though, right?" she asked anxiously, the hearts suspended on springs over her festive headband bobbing.

"Nope, not today. I'm grabbing a sandwich at Logan's, but I'll have my cell with me so you can call if you have an emergency," I told her.

"Okay," she said, sounding uncertain.

"How about I bring you back a six-inch roast beef with cheddar and a lemonade?" I asked. Her apple cheeks scrunched up as she clapped enthusiastically.

"That would be wonderful, thank you!" she cried, clasping her plump hands together.

Satisfied that the library would survive for an hour without me, I went to my office to grab my purse. When I emerged, Martin was standing by the front doors, waiting for me. He held open the door for me and I headed towards my car, with Martin following close behind.

"I'm looking forward to this," he told me as he buckled in. "I remember how good Logan's fresh lemonade used to be."

"It still is," I said as I started the car and navigated onto the road. "They still make it fresh-squeezed daily."

"Funny how the food in Pinewood Corners is so good, even compared to big city places," he commented.

I shot a sidelong look at him. "Have you lived in a lot of big cities?" I asked, slowing for a pair of teens crossing the street.

"I get around," he answered vaguely. Then he reached out and turned off the radio. "That's better," he sighed.

"Excuse me," I tried to keep tight control over my voice, "what gives you the right to decide to turn off my radio?" I gripped the wheel.

Martin looked genuinely puzzled. "I was just thinking that a little peace and quiet would be nice. Nicer than whatever that woman was singing loudly about."

"That *woman* is Kelly Clarkson. I'll have you know that 'A Moment Like This' was my wedding song."

"You're divorced though, right?" he asked.

I sucked in an audible breath. I was on the verge of pulling over and kicking the man out of my car when he elaborated on his rude statement.

"I just mean that it's probably depressing to listen to that now, you know? That's why I like music without lyrics. Nothing to raise unpleasant emotions." He leaned back and crossed his arms.

"We wouldn't want to feel any emotions, how horrifying," I muttered under my breath.

I took another deep breath and decided that since we were almost at the sandwich shop, I would give him the benefit of the doubt, mostly because I *really* wanted a meatball sub. Maybe he just wasn't used to compromising.

I left the music off and continued towards Logan's. Martin was smart enough not to speak again until we were seated at a two-top bistro table in the corner of the restaurant, sipping our lemonades and waiting for our sandwiches.

"This place looks just like I remember it," Martin remarked, gazing around the small cafe. The shop was packed this time of day, with everyone jamming the counter to place their orders.

I didn't reply, and a moment later, a voice called out "Fifty-two!" over the din of the crowd and I started to rise. Martin reached out and grasped my forearm. His grip was firm and strong. His touch was warm and it made my pulse quicken. I ignored the sensation and pulled my arm away and tried to rise again.

"Relax, I'll grab it," he said, standing and striding towards the counter before I could protest. He returned a few minutes later with two oblong sandwiches wrapped in brown paper adorned with grease spots, and an extra sandwich and lemonade for Agnes. My mouth watered at the sight.

"Thanks," I said as I unwrapped my meatball sub, smoothing the paper down flat like a placemat. The tangy marinara and herb seasoned meatballs smelled divine. I picked up the sandwich carefully and leaned forward over the paper, sinking my teeth into the fresh and soft Italian roll. The melted mozzarella stretched out in a long white ribbon as I bit in and pulled the sandwich away. I closed my eyes and moaned loudly in ecstasy as the caramelized cheese, hearty and juicy meatballs, and the sweet yet spicy marinara filled my mouth.

When I opened my eyes, Martin was eyeing me warily.

"Maybe I should have what you're having," he said.

"Is that a reference to *When Harry Met Sally?*" I teased. Martin looked blank.

"What do you mean?" he asked, genuinely puzzled.

"You know, that famous scene, in Katz's Deli, with Meg Ryan? The 'I'll have what she's having' scene?" Still nothing.

"Is that a movie? I don't see many movies," Martin said.

"Never mind," I replied, shaking my head. I pulled on my straw. "So tell me about these theories you have."

Martin wiped his mouth with a napkin, dabbing oil and vinegar dressing from his beard.

"I found a box of letters that were written between two cousins, dated from October 1865 through December 1866. One of the cousins was named Lilian Hanrahan, and she was writing to a Rosemary Wilimington. Lilian was in Pinewood Corners, and Rosemary was from Pinewood Corners but had moved away after her marriage. The women talk quite a bit about the disappearance of Maeve and her necklace. It was the hot gossip of its day." He paused for a sip of his drink and continued.

"Anyway, Lilian goes into a detailed description of the necklace in one of her letters. She stated that her servant, one Mary Elizabeth O'Grady, described the necklace to her. Now, if you remember—"

"Nobody other than Merrick McKenna and the jewelry designer had ever seen the necklace. But how do you know that this Lilian person wasn't just trying to show off and making it up?"

Martin looked smug. "Because," he said, "her description matches the surviving sketches to a tee."

"Maybe she saw the sketches," I offered.

Martin shook his head. "You're forgetting, this was the mid 1860s," he reasoned. "It's not like today, when just about any image is a Google search away."

I picked up my nearly forgotten sandwich and took another bite, reveling in happiness that the sandwich was just as delicious as I remembered, as I considered Martin's words.

"So what's the next move? You said you wanted to talk to some people in town."

"Well, I can't find anything so far on the mysterious Mary Elizabeth. Servants weren't generally considered important enough to have their journals and correspondence preserved. But I was hoping that Lilian Hanrahan might have descendants in the area that I could talk to. I don't know, maybe they'll have some additional family items that could help me track down more clues."

I fiddled with my straw. "There are still Hanrahans in the area. There's a William Hanrahan in Westlake, the next town over to the east," I said, recalling a library card issued for the bookmobile program that reached outlying areas in the county. The name had stuck in my mind for some reason.

"I did a genealogy, and I've concluded that William Hanrahan in Westlake is a direct descendant of Lilian, the letter-writer," Martin said proudly.

"Then why are you 'bouncing' this off me if you already knew that, and you already intended to speak with Mr. Hanrahan?" I was irritated with him now.

"I wanted to ask for your help, since you're a local. Mr. Hanrahan may be more willing to let me in and speak to me if I have a woman with me—especially a librarian. People feel more comfortable in general around females. And you'd be surprised at how willing people are to talk to someone who is writing a book. Would you be inclined to drive me out to interview him?" Martin leaned back and waited for me to respond. *Ahh, so he needed a ride, did he?*

I took my time, letting him stew. I took another bite of my sandwich, polishing it off. I chewed very slowly and methodically, and washed everything down with the last of my lemonade, slurping the last of the liquid loudly through my straw.

"Be right back, I need a refill for the road," I said, grinning. Martin looked to be on the verge of apoplexy, his cheeks turning purple above his auburn beard.

I strolled to one of the large lemonade jar dispensers along the wall and made a show of carefully prying up the plastic lid on my cup and topping up the ice and the pale yellow lemonade. By the time I returned to the table, there were beads of sweat visible on Martin's forehead.

"I'm very curious, so I will help you," I said. "I'm off tomorrow, so I'll drive us to Westlake to speak with William Hanrahan."

Martin let out all his breath in a *whoosh* and slumped in his seat with relief.

"Pick me up at the B&B at 8 a.m.?"

"Make it nine and you've got a deal," I said. He reached out to shake on it.

Before I took his hand, I said, "And to quote one of my favorite TV shows, 'The driver picks the music, shotgun shuts his cakehole.'" I gripped his hand and shook firmly.

"What show is *that?*"

"*Supernatural.*" I winked.

"You are a strange woman." Martin eyed me warily.

"And proud of it." I turned on my heels and walked out with my nose in the air, leaving Martin to follow me.

Chapter four

"Mama, why is Anna gonna marry that guy? He's a bad guy! She needs to marry Kristoff." Claire looked up at me, her wide green eyes, so like my own, questioning the character's motives.

After a dinner of beef stew from the slow cooker and some fresh sourdough rolls, courtesy of my best friend Mikki, we spent the evening watching *Frozen,* one of Claire's favorite movies. I took a deep breath and prepared to explain, for what felt like the hundredth time.

"Honey, she doesn't know yet that he's a bad guy. He hasn't shown his true self yet," I said as I stroked her hair. "You know that she will find out who he truly is before it's too late, and then she won't marry him."

"So he's telling a lie?" she asked, tipping her head to the side.

"Yes, sort of," I told her. I rose and clicked off the TV. "Time for teeth and bed," I said. This prompted a pouting and stomping fit, which was par for the course. Since the divorce, every night when bedtime rolled around, it was a big fight.

It always went in stages. The first stage was denial. She would act like it couldn't possibly be bedtime, and she would refuse to accept the terms. The second stage was fight or flight. She would slip away and try to hide, or simply tell me "no" because she wasn't tired. The third stage was bargaining. If she was allowed to stay up late, she would clean her room and eat all her dinner, forever and ever. Since I always refused to bargain, she would eventually reach the final stage of acceptance and consent to brushing her teeth before climbing into her frilly pink-and-white canopy bed.

Now she lay on her *Frozen* themed sheets and gazed up at me, her blonde hair a nimbus around her head, looking for all the world like a perfect angel that never misbehaved or argued.

"What story would you like to hear tonight?" I asked her, gesturing to her bookcase with its extensive collection of children's books. She was the daughter of a librarian, after all.

"I wanna hear the story about how you and Daddy met." Her little hands clutched the top of the comforter. I abandoned the bookcase and came to sit at the foot of her bed.

"Well, your daddy and I went to school together. One day, after algebra class, he came up to me in the hallway and asked me what I was doing after school that day, and since the English lit book club was canceled that day, he invited me to hang out with him and his friends at the ice cream shop. Then he asked me to sit at his friends' table with him in the cafeteria during lunchtime. We hung around together and were good friends for a long, long time, until your daddy gave me a kiss and asked me to be his girlfriend."

Claire sat up, clapping her hands in excitement. "And then you and my daddy got married, and I was borned." She beamed at me. "And you were your true selfs!"

"Selves." I automatically corrected her. Her statement gave me pause. *Was I really my "true self" in my relationship with Jed?* I leaned down and gave Claire a kiss.

"Now it's time to lie down and close your eyes, sweetheart."

Claire begged for another story, but I insisted on lights out. I turned her little Elsa night light on and shut off the ceiling light at the switch.

"Good night, Claire-bear. Sweet dreams."

"Goodnight, Mama." She rolled onto her side, and I pulled the door half-closed.

I headed for the kitchen to make a cup of tea. I filled the electric kettle with water and chose my favorite mug. It was over-sized and painted in a colorful tie-dye inspired pattern, with swirls of teal, pink, yellow, purple, and orange.

I absolutely loved vibrant colors and rich patterns and textures. In my role as head librarian, I maintained an understated and conservative look with my clothes and jewelry, but in my home life, I indulged my fondness for bright and colorful things. Mikki used to call me "Hippie Gypsy" back in junior high. Jed had always said that my preferred style was "gaudy."

Come to think of it, I had toned my look way down once Jed and I started dating. I could tell he was embarrassed by my long, patterned, gypsy-style skirts, silky tank tops, piles of colorful bracelets, beaded sandals, long layered necklaces, and my trailing gauzy scarves that I used to wrap my long unruly curls up into. While he had never explicitly asked me to stop dressing in boho style clothes, he had definitely made it clear that he thought I looked better in the bland, more neutral styles that were popular at the time.

Lost in thought, I poured the boiling water over the peppermint and chamomile tea bag that dangled inside my cup. The steam bathed my face and I breathed deeply, inhaling the calm and refreshing minty-apple scent.

I opened the red and pink bakery box that Mikki had left at the library's front desk for me earlier. To my delight, it contained a half-dozen small square cakes covered in various chocolate and white coatings decorated with pink and white icing stripes criss-crossing the cakes like ribbons, with little icing bows in the center. I picked up the note that was included.

Hey bestie, I'm working on some new petit fours for the bakery to highlight the Sweetheart Soiree festival. Let me know what you think! Love, Mikki

I chose a white-coated cake with a pink icing ribbon and bow. I bit through the soft coating and into layers of white cake and what tasted like passion fruit and custard cream filling. I leaned against the counter and closed my eyes, allowing myself to be in the moment and fully enjoy the confection as the sweetness and tartness and creamy texture flooded my tongue. It was exquisite.

In the interest of being thorough, I selected a dark chocolate-enrobed treat next. The ganache was covering fudge cake and raspberry filling, and it was so rich and luscious that I needed a sip of tea to wash it down. I grabbed my phone and texted Mikki. *Hey, girl! LOVED the petit fours! You've got a winner, 10 out of 10!* I added a drooling emoji and a thumbs up.

I carried my mug into the living room, intending to start reading a copy of a new hard back mystery novel that the library had received that morning. One of the benefits of working at the library was reading all the latest novels first.

I settled on the sofa with my thick magenta blanket and cuddled into the softness and warmth. Instead of reaching for the book, however, I found myself reaching for my journal. I pulled the pen from its elastic loop and opened the book to the next blank spot, jotted the date, and began to pour my thoughts out onto the page.

Tonight when I was putting Claire to bed, she said something about how Jed and I were our true selves together when we got married. I can't get it out of my mind now.

Was I my true self? Was Jed? I think back on how very young we were when we got married. Maybe we were as true to ourselves as we could be at that age, but then we grew up. Jed proposed during our high school graduation party, in front of our families and our friends, and I ecstatically accepted.

I thought my life was working out perfectly according to plan. That plan was to get married, attend college, become a librarian, start a family … and yet, life threw me a curveball. My "perfect life" was upended. And by me, no less.

I've always told myself that we split because the passion died, and that in itself is true. But now I'm starting to question exactly why the passion died. When did it get to a point of no return? Why didn't I want to fix it?

I look around my house, the house I used to share with Jed, and real-ize that it's almost unrecognizable from the way it looked when Jed lived here. I got rid of or revamped the bland and boring stuff and decorated my home with the vibrant and rich fabrics and colors and textures that I've always loved. Now I question if I even knew who my "true self" was during my marriage.

How much of myself did I suppress and compromise in order to be the wife I thought I was supposed to be? The wife Jed wanted me to be? Did I sabotage my own marriage in order to escape? To be free to express my true self before I lost touch with her forever?

Hiding your own needs and pretending to be someone else is a recipe for resentment down the line. These thoughts are haunting my mind now. I don't know if I will ever have the answers about my marriage, but I do know that I very much like the woman I am today, and I will not subdue myself like that again.

If (when!) I open myself to another relationship, I vow that I will refuse to blunt anything about myself merely because it might please my partner. I've worked hard to find myself, and it scares me to think that I could lose her again in another relationship. Will opening my heart close my connection to myself? Is it inevitable that I must lose myself to love another?

I closed the book and my eyes felt heavy with fatigue and unshed tears. I squeezed them shut and took a few deep, cleansing breaths. I sipped my lukewarm tea as I reflected on my insights.

Maybe I should have tried harder with Jed, but that ship had sailed long ago. Even if he showed up at my door right now and begged me to take him back, I would not want that.

But what, exactly, *did* I want?

Passion. Chemistry. Support. Adventure. Trust. Acceptance. It sounded so simple and yet so vague, so appealing, and yet so hard to find.

I swallowed the last of my tea and headed for bed, leaving the empty mug on the coffee table.

*   *   *

It was twelve minutes after nine when I pulled up in front of the PC B&B the next morning. Martin was standing on the sidewalk in front of the building, looking at his watch. This was getting to be a habit.

When he saw my car, he splayed his gloved hands up and out, in a "finally" gesture. He approached the passenger side door and yanked the handle. When the door didn't open, he peered through the window at me, scowling from under his black knit cap.

I hit the button to unlock the door, and he immediately wrenched the door open and plopped into the passenger seat.

"It's freezing out there," he grumbled, rubbing his hands together in front of the heater vent. "And you're late."

"I had to drop my daughter off, and there was some issue with payment at the preschool that took longer to resolve than I expected. I got here as quickly as I could." I glanced over at him before pulling back onto the road. "You didn't have to wait outside, you know."

"I know, but I realized that you don't have my number so I thought it would be prudent to wait outside so you wouldn't have to get out of the car when you arrived."

"Oh. I guess that makes sense," I said. "We should probably exchange numbers if I'm going to continue chauffeuring you around town during your visit." I looked in the side mirror to check for traffic and rolled out into the street.

As Martin shifted around, pulling on his seatbelt, he bumped some papers in the compartment above the glove box, and a folded pink flier drifted onto his lap.

He picked it up and unfolded it, studying the hearts and arrows around the border. It was a flier promoting the library's love poetry contest. After staring at the page for a few moments, he re-folded the paper and replaced it in the compartment.

"What's Cupid's Ball?" he asked.

"Weren't you around for it?"

"No, I was only here over the summers, and sometimes for Thanksgiving or Christmas. By the time Valentine's Day rolled around, I was back at my mom's house and school was in session."

"Makes sense," I said. "Cupid's Ball is a formal dance that is the culmination of the Sweetheart Soiree festival. Most of the festival consists of local merchants having themed sales, some cute booths selling specialty Valentine's themed merchandise, wine and chocolate tastings and a kissing booth for the adults and craft booths for the children, caricature artists, that sort of thing. There's even a Cupid's arrow archery contest. But the Cupid's Ball is something everyone looks forward to. Everyone gets dressed up and dances the night away. It's second only to the Halloween Harvest Masquerade Ball in October in popularity."

"So it's kind of like prom for adults?" Martin asked.

"Yes, I suppose it is rather like that," I admitted. Silence descended for a few minutes.

"That's an interesting outfit," Martin remarked as he glanced at me. I was wearing a long purple skirt patterned with yellow paisley designs and a hint of gold sequins, with purple suede boots and a yellow fuzzy sweater. I decided to take his words as a compliment.

"Thank you," I said. "Some people think my personal style is too much."

Martin lifted one shoulder. "Fashion is irrelevant to me. I only noticed your outfit because it's unusual." He opened the carryall at his feet and extracted a small notebook that he flipped through.

"Go to Highway 46 and head north."

"I know how to get to Westlake," I said caustically. I had lived in the area since I was a child, after all.

"Right," Martin said, unaffected by my tone. "I'll just give you the exact address as we get closer and you can plug it into your maps app."

He dropped the notebook into his bag and settled in and closed his eyes. After a few miles, I found the quiet to be somewhat unnerving, so I reached over and flipped on the radio.

One of my playlists connected to the car's bluetooth and Fleetwood Mac's "Rhiannon" began to play. I glanced over to see Martin's reaction.

He opened one eye and narrowed it. His chest rose and fell with what I could only assume was a deep and calming breath, and then he surprised me by closing his eyes again and not saying a word.

"Rhi-aaaaaaaa-non," I sang out as I merged onto the highway and headed towards Westlake. Martin simply pulled his beanie lower over his ears.

As I eased my blue sedan over to the inside lane, I noticed a small white car, low and sleek, sliding over into the lane behind me. It looked like the same Dodge Avenger that had tailgated me and flown past the night we had stopped at the El for dinner. Since there were a lot of white cars on the road, I didn't dwell on it and kept my attention on the road in front of me.

We stopped for a snack and a bathroom break halfway there, and Martin typed his number into my phone, as well as the address of William Hanrahan, as we leaned together on the hood of my car. I squinted at the map on the screen.

"Does this guy know we're coming, or are we about to ambush someone?" I asked Martin.

"I called and spoke with him yesterday afternoon. I couldn't risk driving all the way out there and having him be out. I would lose too much time." He popped the last of his cherry danish into his mouth and tossed the wrapper into the trash can before climbing into the car. He sat there, staring forward while I guzzled the last of my coffee before joining him.

Once we were back on the road, I relaxed in the comfort of the warm car. I turned down the volume on the radio, muting Tom Petty's "American Girl." Martin looked relieved but tried to cover it up with a cough.

"So, tell me a little about yourself," I began. "Where do you live when you're not in Pinewood Corners?"

He took his time responding, uncapping his water bottle and taking a long drink before he spoke.

"I'm sort of a vagabond. I have a Master's degree in archeology, with a BA in history. I sometimes have teaching gigs for a semester or two, when I'm not on location for a dig somewhere. I tend to live wherever my current project is."

I felt myself stiffen at the mention of archeology, my hands gripping the wheel so tightly that my knuckles turned white.

Martin, surprisingly sensitive to my reaction, asked, "Did I say something wrong?"

I swallowed and took in a deep breath. "No, I … I think I drank that coffee too fast and the caffeine is hitting me hard." I managed a shaky laugh and tried to relax my hold on the steering wheel. Martin looked skeptical, but he didn't push for any further explanations.

"Anyway," he continued, "I was between gigs and decided to start a book, the one on lost treasures in America, and then my dad got engaged, so I figured this was the perfect opportunity to come to Pinewood Corners and conduct research for the book and attend the wedding. Two birds, one stone." He sat back, looking pleased with himself.

"You seem in a hurry to get your research done," I observed. "When are you leaving town?"

"Right after the wedding," he replied. "I have an opportunity to participate in a dig in southeastern Mexico at the end of February."

"Southeastern Mexico? As in the Yucatan Peninsula?" The white-knuckled grip had returned.

"That's right," Martin said. "I specialize in ancient Mesoamerican civilizations. I've been down there many times before."

I tried to calm myself down. Just because my parents disappeared in the Yucatan Mountains years ago didn't mean anything was going to happen to Martin there. He just said he'd been down there many times, for goodness sakes. It wasn't exactly the Bermuda Triangle. Besides, I didn't even really know Martin well enough to justify such a strong reaction, I told myself.

I forced a smile. "That sounds great." I lied. Desperate to change the subject, I asked, "Have you ever been married?"

"My career interests don't exactly create an ideal environment for a marriage. I travel so much, I'm never in one place for long," he said. "I got close once. I even bought her a ring and proposed, but …" Martin trailed off.

Just then, a disembodied voice from my phone announced that I should exit the highway in two miles. I began glancing in the rearview mirror and working my way over to the far right lane to make my exit. I noticed what appeared to be the same white Dodge behind me. *It has to be a coincidence,* I thought to myself. After all, why would anyone want to follow me? The thought seemed ridiculous.

I continued to follow the directions voiced by the phone's navigation app, and before long we pulled up in front of a small Craftsman style bungalow with dark green paint and creamy white accents.

"Let me do the talking," Martin advised as he unclipped his seat belt and grabbed his messenger bag.

"I will do no such thing," I said, climbing out of the car. With a put-upon sigh, Martin followed me up the path and onto the porch. He reached around me and pushed the doorbell.

The sound of multiple barking dogs exploded from inside the house. A man's voice yelled, "Hush, all of you! Outside!"

A door slammed from within and then the barking horde could be heard echoing through the chilled morning air.

Footsteps approached, and the heavy, shiny white front door swung open. A portly man with wispy white hair and black-framed glasses stood in the doorway, blinking at us.

"Hello, sir," Martin stepped forward, hand extended. "We spoke on the phone last night. I'm Martin Weaver." The man shook his hand and glanced at me.

"Hello, you must be Mr. Hanrahan. I'm Lacey Crawford. I run the library in Pinewood Corners," I said, smiling warmly.

The man grinned back, his yellowed dentures on full display. "Please call me Bill," he said, stepping aside and opening the door wider. "Come in, come in, and make yourselves comfortable."

We stepped inside and the pungent smell of dogs in the close and stuffy air overwhelmed me. I barely managed to suppress a gasp. I glanced at Martin and saw that his eyes were watering. Bill gestured to a long gray couch against the wall under the front windows.

"Have a seat, you two. I've got a pot of tea brewing, I'll just go and fetch it now." He hurried from the room.

Martin and I approached the couch, picking our way over the multitude of dog toys and chewed rawhide bits that littered the floor. It was absolutely covered in dog hair.

I looked at Martin, panic in my eyes. "I can't sit on that!" I hissed in a loud whisper.

"You have two dogs!"

"Yes, and I also have a vacuum cleaner, a hand vacuum, *and* a pet hair roller that I use multiple times a week to get rid of dog hair on the furniture!"

Martin put out his hand, palm down, lowering it slowly in a *calm down* motion. Wordlessly, he slipped out of his coat and laid it across one of the cushions and waved his hand to indicate that I should sit on the coat. I did so, perching as close to the edge as I could without falling off. Martin rolled his eyes and took a seat on the opposite side of the couch.

Bill came shuffling into the room, barely balancing a tray with a black cast-iron teapot, three ceramic cups, and a sugar bowl.

"If you want milk, I think I may have some in the back of the fridge somewhere," he said, as Martin jumped up to help him with the tray.

"Uh, thanks, this will be fine," I replied, thinking that any milk this man may have in the back of the fridge probably expired around the time I graduated from college.

I noticed that there was dog hair floating in my cup. I pretended to take a sip. "Mmmm," I murmured, because Bill seemed to be watching me for a reaction.

Martin appeared to have no trepidation about drinking dog hair and was happily sipping away. I shuddered and placed my cup into the saucer on the coffee table.

"Now, what's this about some old letters from my ancestor?" Bill asked. I appreciated that he was getting right to the point.

Martin put his teacup down and leaned forward, warming to his subject. "As I said on the phone, I'm writing a book on lost treasures in America, and I'm in the area researching the legend of the missing wife of the founder of Pinewood Corners, Maeve McKenna, and her lost necklace."

"Oh, yes, I know that story," Bill said. "But how does that pertain to me?"

"Well, in the course of my research, I came across some letters written by a Lilian Hanrahan. I believe she is a direct ancestor of yours," Martin replied.

Bill nodded his head thoughtfully. "Yes, she's my great-great-great aunt, according to the family tree. I dragged out some of the old paperwork after our telephone conversation. Lilian did live in Pinewood Corners back in the day when Mrs. McKenna went missing. The family fortunes were much larger in those days," he said, sounding apologetic.

I wasn't sure how to respond to that, so I just smiled and turned to Martin, who continued speaking.

"What I'm hoping to find is more letters, or family papers, or something like that, that you might have in your possession."

Bill looked thoughtful. Suddenly, the back door thudded loudly and rattled as something solid slammed into it from outside. I let out a little shriek as I jumped in surprise and a volley of barking rang out. Bill ignored the dogs and turned to me.

"Ma'am, I just want to say thank you for the bookmobile program," he said. "It's only me here, and my dogs of course, and without the bookmobile, I would have to drive all the way out to Pinewood Corners to check out my spy thriller novels."

"Oh, you're welcome. It's so nice to hear that the book-mobile is being utilized by your community," I responded, smiling at Bill.

Martin interrupted our warm exchange by clearing his throat. "Yes, that's very nice. Now, back to Lilian. If you by chance have any boxes of letters, journals, or maybe an old family Bible, that sort of thing, it could prove very helpful in my research," he said.

"I do think I have some things you may be interested in," Bill responded. "There are several boxes of family papers in the spare room closet. They've been collecting dust for years. My children aren't the least bit interested in them, and the historical society didn't seem to want them. I would love to pass them along to such distinguished scholars as yourselves."

I thought he was being overly generous in his description of us, but I kept my thoughts to myself. Martin, on the other hand, was practically vibrating with excitement.

"Wonderful! I'm happy to help you carry them," he offered.

"I'd appreciate that, young man," Bill replied. Martin followed him as he went down a hallway off the living room.

I stayed put. A thick, velvety layer of dust and dog hair coated every surface of the room. Before me sat an ancient, hulking console model television, with an elaborately carved wood casing. In the corner, a fireplace with beautiful built-in bookshelves beckoned me over. I couldn't resist the allure of books.

Walking over to investigate, I noticed most of them were old *Reader's Digest* condensed novels. Unimpressed, I was about to sit down again when Martin returned, carrying two cartons stacked atop one another. Bill had a third carton. I hurried to take it from him.

"Here, let me help you with that," I said. He relinquished the carton and pulled a yellowed handkerchief from his pocket and wiped his brow.

"Thank you, ma'am. The older I get, the heavier everything seems to be," Bill said.

"Well, I guess we should let you get back to your day. We'll just head out now so I can get started going through these," Martin said. He sat the boxes down, collected his coat, and held out his hand.

"Thank you, Bill. If I find anything of significance, I will let you know." Bill shook Martin's hand and wished us both a good day.

We deposited the three boxes into the trunk of my car and got on the road. Martin was so excited about his find that he didn't even react when I started the car and "Crazy in Love" by Beyoncé blasted from the speakers. I turned the volume even higher as I hit the gas and headed for home.

Chapter five

"This could be huge. I mean, this could break things wide open," Martin said for what seemed like the hundredth time. His amber eyes shone with excitement and he was fidgeting as though he could barely stay confined by his seatbelt.

"Look," I cautioned him, "the information in those boxes *might* be groundbreaking, but it may also be just a pile of old greeting cards and expired coupons."

Martin sighed heavily. "I know, you're right, but I prefer to think positively. In this profession, it's easy to get excited with very little provocation." He shifted in his seat again. "Once, I saw a group of people get so giddy over finding a tiny little pewter button on a dig that they celebrated by going on a three-day bender over it. There's precious little physical evidence left of our history, so every morsel matters."

"You're really passionate about this sort of thing," I observed as I turned on my signal and started moving the car towards the far right lane to take my exit.

Martin didn't reply, as he was too busy rummaging in the bag at his feet. He sat up, clutching a small notebook. As we pulled up to the traffic light, I glanced over at him. He was scribbling away, deep in concentration. I had turned the music down for our conversation and now I reached over and turned it up again, just to see how Martin would react.

As the tones of Mariah Carey's 90s hit "Fantasy" rose from the speakers, Martin briefly glanced up at me, rolled his eyes, and quickly shifted his focus back to the notebook.

"What's in the book?" I asked, pitching my voice higher to speak over Mariah.

"My notes and ideas, items I want to follow up on, that sort of thing," Martin shouted back. "You know, we wouldn't have to shout if you'd turn that noise down."

Martin brought out the petulant side of me for reasons I couldn't begin to comprehend, and I stubbornly set my lips in a firm line and turned the volume up another notch. Martin shook his head and returned to his furious note-taking.

The light turned green and I spun the wheel as I turned onto Oak Boulevard. The song ended, and I reluctantly turned the volume down.

"Am I dropping you off at the B&B?" I asked.

Martin hesitated. "I don't have much space to spread out in my room there, just the bed and a small secretary's desk. Maybe you could drop me at the library, and I could work there?"

I shook my head. "I don't think it's a good idea for you to bring all those boxes of papers and whatnot in there. What if there are bugs in them? I don't need my library infested with bugs!" I shuddered dramatically. "Besides, the library will be closing in an hour."

"Oh for the love of—" Martin closed his mouth before he could put his foot deeper into it. On a sudden impulse, I yanked the steering wheel abruptly and swung the car into the parking lot of O'Shanty's, the local bar and grill. As I did, a white Dodge Avenger raced past. It looked like the one that had nearly clipped my rear bumper. I wondered if it might be the same car. *What an aggressive driver!*

"What are you doing?" Martin asked, his tone more curious than demanding.

"I'm hungry. Late lunch, early dinner, take your pick. I need a root beer. They have it on tap here." I shoved the door open and stepped out, taking in a lungful of the crisp, icy air. It felt bracing after the warm and stuffy atmosphere of the car. I turned back to look at Martin, sitting in the passenger seat, still belted in and blinking at me like a puzzled owl.

"Are you coming?" I didn't wait for him to answer as I slammed the driver's side door shut and stalked towards the door of the building with a toss of my hair over my shoulder.

I heard the metallic squawk of the passenger door opening and the slam of it closing, followed by the crunch of Martin's low boots on the gravel. Moving with surprising speed and grace, he shot past me and grabbed the worn brass door handle, pulling it open and gesturing me inside with a deep bow.

Laughing, I swatted him with the end of my scarf as I walked past him. The dimly lit room was a sharp contrast to the bright and glaring overcast winter day outside. The air itself seemed to carry grease particles straight into my nostrils. I sucked a deep dose in through my nose and opened my mouth to exhale forcefully.

"Ahh! Nothing like the O'Shanty's dining room," I said fondly.

"I think my cholesterol levels just went up from breathing," Martin remarked with a grimace. "Shall we adjourn to a booth, m'lady?" he asked.

There were plenty of open tables and booths this early in the day. I knew that later in the evening, the bar would be packed with patrons that wanted a cocktail, a game of pool, or some dancing and socializing. On the weekends, O'Shanty's offered live music. It was fun, even if it was usually just Dr. Griffon, the town's veterinarian, and his cousin, Brady, playing their guitars.

As we slid into a booth—quite literally, as the vinyl bench seats were shiny with grease and extensive use—a young and perky blonde woman approached us.

"Hey, Lacey!" Her eyes traveled to Martin. "And who might this be?"

"Hi, Linda," I replied. Linda Cranston, sister to the sheriff's dispatcher Mindy, smiled so widely that I thought she might split her head in two.

"I'm Martin," Martin said with a nod of acknowledgment to her.

"Pleased to meet you, I'm Linda," Linda purred, somehow grinning even wider. " Would you like some waters to start?" She placed two stained paper menus on the table.

"Sure, that sounds good," I replied. As Linda disappeared, I picked up my menu and studied it. Martin did the same.

"I've been indulging a little too much lately. Maybe I'll have a salad," he mused.

I was alarmed. "You don't want to do that," I warned him.

"Why not? It's a simple salad. How could anyone mess that up?" he scoffed.

"You'd be surprised."

Linda returned with two glasses of water and set them on the table. "You two ready to order?" she asked, whipping an order pad from her apron pocket.

"I'll have the deep fried hot dog, with cheese, on the toasted potato bun, curly fries, and a large root beer, please," I said as I handed the menu back to her. Linda turned to Martin expectantly, her pen poised over the order pad.

"I'll have the chef's salad, please, with the dressing on the side," he said. "And the water is fine."

"Okay, sounds great," Linda said. She disappeared again to put in our orders. I picked up my water glass and sipped at the tepid liquid. Martin sat across from me in silence, looking pensively at the wall behind my head.

"Penny for your thoughts," I said. Martin's eyes shifted to focus on my face.

"I'm just trying to think about where to land. I guess I'll call my dad and see if I can hang out at his place for a while so I can go through those boxes," he said.

"Why aren't you staying there?" I asked, and immediately regretted asking such a nosy question.

"I wanted to give my dad space, he's preparing for his wedding and all that," Martin replied with a shrug. He didn't seem offended at my curiosity.

"Look, bugs notwithstanding, I will admit that I'm fairly interested in what might be in those boxes. Why don't you bring them to my house? I'd ask that you camp out on the back porch, just in case."

"Back porch? But it's cold," Martin protested.

I waved him off. "It's enclosed. You can bring the papers in as we sort through them."

Martin leaned back in the booth. "Okay, I agree to your terms. I'll admit that you're more qualified to help me sort through papers than my dad."

"Wow, what a ringing endorsement," I said flatly.

"Here we go!" Linda sang as she placed a giant frosted mug of root beer on the table in front of me. "I'll be back in a jiffy with your meals." She hurried off towards the kitchen.

I leaned forward and placed my lips on the rim of the tall mug and slurped the foam off the top of the brew. Martin's face screwed up in revulsion.

"Don't you like my table manners?" I asked in an innocent tone, blinking at him. He surprised me by tossing his head back and laughing heartily. I liked the sound of his laugh, high and loud and barking. I grinned as I unwrapped my straw and plunged it into the mug of root beer.

Linda returned with a plate in each hand and plunked them down in front of us. "Enjoy!" she chirped and wandered off towards the bar.

Martin stared down at his plate while I pushed up my sleeves in preparation for picking up my hot dog, dripping with vivid-yellow cheese sauce.

"What is it?" he asked. His voice was incredulous with horror. I wasn't sure if he was referring to my hot dog or to his so-called salad.

"This, my friend, is a hot dog that has been deep fried and tucked into a buttered and toasted potato bun and topped with the kind of cheese sauce that's always in a liquid state and comes in a giant can." I pointed to his plate. "You have before you a plate of brown and white wilted iceberg lettuce covered with bits of pimento loaf lunch meat, a blob of relish, and hard boiled eggs with green yolks, and for your topping pleasure, some ranch dressing on the side."

Martin blanched and pushed the plate away. I took pity on him and offered him my fries, which he happily accepted.

"You should try the root beer, too," I said as I pushed the mug his way. He gingerly sipped from the rim and experimentally swirled the drink around his mouth, swallowed, and immediately went for another long drink.

"Do you want to order one?"

He shook his head. "Just another straw, if you don't mind. We can share."

Absurdly pleased, I asked a passing server for a second straw and plunged it into the root beer next to my own. I felt like we were a couple of teenagers from the 1950s.

Martin popped another French fry into his mouth.

"Are we going straight to your place after this?" he asked.

I reddened as Linda approached the table with our check. I knew she had heard what Martin had asked me, and it sounded like a very risqué question out of context. I tried to nip the rumor mill in the bud.

"Well, I do have a couple of errands to run before I'll be able to return to my house so that we can continue doing research," I said loudly for Linda's benefit.

"Doing research? Is that what they're calling it these days?" Linda asked cattily as she tore the check off the pad and placed it on the table between Martin and me, grinning lasciviously.

"I'm sure I don't know what you're talking about," I said frostily as I handed her my debit card. "It's on me, and please take the salad off the bill. Martin wasn't able to eat it."

"Fine," Linda said, snatching the credit card out of my hand.

"You didn't have to do that," Martin said, watching the shapely Linda walk away.

"Well, it certainly improved the view for you," I snapped. Martin raised his eyebrows but didn't say anything. As soon as Linda returned with my card, I scrawled a tip on the line and signed the slip. I was irritated with myself for having a jealous flare-up.

"Let's go," I said, sliding out of the booth. Martin followed me through the front doors and sucked in a deep breath as soon as we were outside.

"Fresh air at last," he remarked.

"At least it smelled better than wet dogs in there," I quipped.

Martin gave a short laugh as we climbed into the car.

"Do you really have errands, or were you just saying that?" he asked as he buckled his seat belt.

"I really do need to pick up some dog food. My ex is dropping Claire off after dinner tonight, but I should also run by the Fresh Stop and get some milk, bread, and cereal."

Martin looked at his chunky analog watch. "It's still fairly early. I'm happy to accompany you on your errands."

"Thanks a lot, Sir Galahad," I said wryly, and I was rewarded with another one of Martin's barking laughs. I tried to hide my smile as we pulled out of the parking lot.

*   *   *

The Pet Palace always smelled very earthy, like fermented wheat. I didn't know if it was the various types of pet food on the shelves, the fish tanks lining the rear wall, or the cages of small reptiles and mammals, or a combination of everything that caused the smell that permeated the air in the store.

"Hi, Lacey! I see you have a new friend, eh?" Colleen Perkins, a cheerful blonde woman who had worked at the Pet Palace for as long as I could recall, greeted us with the now-familiar refrain. Colleen wore a red apron with the Pet Palace logo plastered across the bib over jeans and a tan sweatshirt. Her hair was cut short around the back and sides, leaving the top longer and it curled atop the crown of her head. I knew she was a natural blonde but had the top of her hair permed because we both had our hair cut by the same stylist. The same gossipy stylist.

I introduced Martin to Colleen. She gave him a wide smile as she pumped his hand up and down. "Hi, I'm Colleen. Are you new to Pinewood Corners? I've lived here all my life, I just love it here. My family goes way back. But I'm the last of the line, or so I'm told. Single, too, no kids. I would love to have them someday, though. Do you have kids? They're just wonderful. Anyway, this is a great town. There's a festival to celebrate nearly every season, and it just makes the whole year feel special, don't you think so? I think so. And the people are so friendly, and the food here is wonderful. Welcome to Pinewood Corners! Are you looking to adopt a pet? We have lots of fish, birds and reptiles and small mammals. We don't have cats or dogs here, but the county runs a great shelter where you can adopt a cat or a dog. We do have food for cats and dogs here, just not the actual cats and dogs. And—"

"I'm just here to pick up a bag of dog food for Jethro and Elly May," I cut in. I knew from experience that if you waited for Colleen to wind down before speaking, you'd be waiting a good, long while. Colleen finally stopped yanking Martin's hand up and down and released him.

"Oh, sure, of course. Your dogs are so cute! Right this way," Colleen bustled down one of the aisles to point out the brand of dog food I preferred. Martin leaned down and scooped up the large bag of kibble and tossed it over his shoulder.

"Anything else?" he asked, raising his eyebrows at me.

"I did want to grab some dog biscuits," I reached out and grabbed the nearest box of dog treats and then led the way to the register at the front of the shop, where Colleen scanned my items. I tapped my phone to pay and we were on our way.

"On to the Fresh Stop," I said as I started up the car. Martin leaned back in his seat and closed his eyes again.

"Wake me when we get there," he mumbled.

"Why do you try to sleep in the car so often? Is my driving that frightening?"

Martin opened one eye. "No, I just developed the habit of grabbing some rest at any opportunity. It's a practice I developed from being on digs. You work for days straight sometimes, and the only rest you get is a few minutes here and there." He closed his eyes and settled down again.

I wonder if my parents had this same habit? I knew so little about them, just bits and pieces, really. I was so young when they disappeared.

As I pulled into a parking spot at the Fresh Stop, the largest grocery store in Pinewood Corners, I clicked the radio off and turned to Martin.

"Wake up, princess, we're here. And be warned, we'll probably run into at least half a dozen locals in there, and they'll all be curious and want to meet you and chat you up."

Martin stirred and shook his head, like a dog shaking off water. "Thanks for the warning. Must be pretty serious, you even turned off Sheryl Crow."

"I can't believe you knew that was her," I said, pleasantly surprised.

"The name of the artist and the song is displayed on the front panel of the radio," Martin replied, pointing at the dashboard.

My bubble effectively burst, I exited the car and stalked towards the entrance to the store. The front windows of the grocery store had been painted with hearts and cupids. Buckets filled with cut roses of every imaginable color lined the covered front entrance. Red, pink, and silver heart-shaped mylar balloons floated above the buckets, swaying gently in the late afternoon breeze. The community billboard was filled with posters and fliers advertising various events and goods and services, most related to the Sweetheart Soiree festival.

Martin stopped in front of the cork board display and studied its contents.

"Thinking of signing up for the kissing booth?" I teased.

"Sweet mercy, no!" Martin's features narrowed so deeply with distaste that it was funny and I laughed in spite of my foul mood.

"I am simply studying the local customs. It's fascinating to me as a student of cultures both present and past. I *am* an archeologist, after all."

I continued into the store, purposely ignoring his comment. I went to the bank of shopping carts and grasped the handle of the nearest one. It was stuck. I stood there yanking on the handle to no avail, until a hand reached around me and grasped the cart.

I could smell bourbon and cherry tobacco and moss. I inhaled deeply and turned around to find myself standing encircled by Martin's arms as he grasped the cart handle. I could feel heat working its way to the surface of my skin, rising from my core with every beat of my heart. Beads of sweat popped out over my upper lip and around my hairline. I inhaled sharply and Martin's amber-gold eyes widened as they locked with mine. I felt as if I were swimming in the golden flecks of his irises, swimming and sinking all at once. Then Martin blinked and the spell was abruptly broken.

"Excuse me," I mumbled and tried to step away. I winced as the cart jabbed into my back.

"Just trying to help," Martin said brusquely. The now freed cart rolled backwards a few inches. I grasped the handle like a lifeline, my knuckles turning white at the pressure.

"Thanks," I said over my shoulder as I walked deeper into the store, leaving Martin to follow. I couldn't bring myself to look directly at him yet. I could hear his footsteps on the linoleum behind me as I headed towards the rear of the store where the dairy items were kept.

As I whipped around the end of the canned goods aisle, I nearly plowed my cart right into another shopper's cart. I pulled up short just in time to avoid a collision and muttered an apology as I looked up into the face of Joanna Morton, my best friend Mikki's grandmother, and future bride to Martin's father, Sheriff Weaver.

Jo looked radiant in her bright red woolen coat, and draped around her neck was a jaunty red scarf covered in tiny red hearts. Red enameled heart earrings dangled from her ears and set off the red frames of her glasses. I smiled to myself. Joanna Morton had always been one of the most festive people in Pinewood Corners, and that was definitely saying something.

Jo beamed at me, her blue eyes sparkling. "Why, Lacey, hello! It's so nice to run into you!" Her gaze traveled to the space behind me. "My you look familiar, hon, do I know you?"

"This," I said, pointing to the general space behind me, "is Martin Weaver, your future son-in-law."

"Oh, yes, of course. It's been a long while since I've seen you, Martin. Your beard has grown since we had that face call to announce the engagement," Jo replied, reaching out to give Martin a quick hug.

Martin smiled, and my pulse quickened at the transformation on his face from pleasant to handsome.

Martin reassured her, placing a hand on Jo's scarlet forearm. "I remember seeing you around from summers here as a boy, but we haven't had a chance to spend much time together since I went off to college."

"Well, then I'm extra glad we ran into each other. Bob did mention that you had come into town a bit earlier than your siblings. He said something about a research project. Your pop is so proud of you, Martin."

What I could see of Martin's face under the beard and the hair falling over his forehead slowly flushed red. "Thanks," he mumbled. "It's really nice seeing you again."

I turned back to Jo. "You know, Martin mentioned that it would be valuable for his project to interview a long-time resident of Pinewood Corners. I thought that you might be the perfect candidate."

Now it was Jo's turn to blush. "Me?" she asked, pointing to her chest, her brows raised. "I've lived here all my life, and if

I know anything that may be of use to you, I would be happy to share it."

"That would be wonderful, if you can spare the time. I know the wedding is coming up soon," Martin said.

"Nonsense, I have everything well in hand," Jo said smugly. "We're exchanging vows at Grace Chapel off Main Street on Valentine's Day, and Mayor Reese is allowing us to celebrate afterwards at the Cupid's Ball in lieu of a traditional reception." Her blue eyes sparkled as her gaze traveled between me and Martin. "Tell you what, why don't you two come to my house for breakfast the day after tomorrow?"

"Absolutely. And thank you," Martin said.

Jo seemed satisfied at that and started up the next aisle. "See you soon, take care, both of you," she said over her shoulder as she walked away to finish her shopping.

Jo had barely disappeared around the corner when another cart came wheeling down the aisle, pushed by a stout brunette woman in a gray uniform complete with a crisp white apron. She stopped the cart and eyed Martin with curiosity.

"Hi, Lacey," she said brightly to me, while never taking her eyes off of Martin. "Have we met?"

"Hi, Erin," I replied. Erin Wells was Mayor Reese's long-time housekeeper, and one of the biggest gossips in Pinewood Corners. I was never going to make it to the dairy case at this rate. I introduced Martin as briefly as I could, merely saying that he was in town for his father's wedding and taking in the festival sights and sounds. I didn't want to give her any information that she might consider interesting enough to repeat to anyone else. Erin bid us goodbye with a disappointed air and moved along.

"Come on, let's get this over with, hurry," I nudged Martin as we hurried towards the back of the store. I grabbed my items quickly, and Martin pulled some fruit cups, protein drinks, and granola bars off the shelves as we flew down the aisles.

"Are you packing lunches for a child?" I teased him.

"No, just stocking up on some easy to store and fairly healthy snacks that don't need to be refrigerated or heated," he replied smoothly.

"Makes sense," I said as I pulled items from the cart and placed them on the black conveyor belt at the checkout stand.

"Hey, Lacey," the cashier said as she began scanning my purchases. It was one of the local high school girls, Brenna Hunt. Brenna's long brown hair was pulled back in a red headband and little cupid-shaped earrings dangled from her earlobes. Brenna efficiently scanned the items and rattled off a total. While I swiped my debit card, Martin stacked his purchases onto the belt.

Brenna handed me the receipt. "Have a great day, Lacey," she told me with a warm smile. She didn't ask who my friend was, to my immense relief. I supposed she was used to seeing strangers come through her line, with all the tourists that came through town for the various festivals. She breezed through Martin's checkout and we headed out to my car.

I opened the door to the backseat to stow the groceries next to Claire's car seat, since my trunk was filled with cartons of papers. I had just settled into the driver's seat and buckled in when my cell phone rang. I glanced at the screen and saw that it was the sheriff's department calling. Alarmed, I swiped the green "accept" button to answer the call.

"Lacey?" It was Mindy Cranston's voice, and she sounded urgent.

Nervously, I answered, "Yes?"

"The library's been broken into, you need to get down there right away!"

Chapter Six

I was such an anxious wreck at the news that Martin insisted I surrender the keys and let him drive us to the library. I was grateful because it gave me the opportunity to call Jed to let him know that I would be late picking Claire up.

"How late will you be? I have a date with Elaine tonight." Jed sounded irritated.

"I don't know, Jed. I just got a call from the sheriff's department that the library has been broken into. I need to get down there and figure out what's going on. I'm not sure what, if any, damage has been done. I"ll know more once I get there." I told him, trying to keep the panic out of my voice. To his credit, Jed calmed down considerably once I informed him of what was going on. He knew how important the library was to me.

"Okay, no worries, you do what you need to do. I can always have Elaine come over here and we can all order a pizza for dinner if it gets too late to go out," he said.

"Thanks, Jed. I'll be in touch as soon as I know something more," I said and then I hit the red button to end the call just as Martin pulled into the library's parking lot. An SUV marked with the county sheriff's department logo was in the lot, red and blue lights flashing and reflecting off the patches of snow that dotted the bushes and grass.

I barely waited for the car to stop rolling before I flung the door open and leapt out, running full tilt for the library's entrance. I collided into the broad and firm chest of Tom Willis, the recently appointed Deputy Sheriff of Pinewood Corners. He reached out and caught my shoulders, keeping me from bouncing off him and falling down.

"Lacey, it's okay, the intruder is gone," he said.

"What happened? Who was it, do you know? Is there any damage?" My words came out in a breathless, shaking rush as tears blurred my vision.

"They broke the glass in your office window, I think that's how they got in. Security cameras inside didn't pick anything up, they just recorded scrambled static. The reference room door was damaged, but they didn't make it in. The glass next to the door has been damaged as well. The silent alarm was triggered, and I came in with lights and sirens. I think that scared the perpetrator away, because the building is clear."

I sagged with relief. "So nothing seems to be taken?" I asked Tom.

"It doesn't look like it to me," Tom said. "You'd be the best judge of that, though."

Martin ambled up at that point, and greeted Tom. They seemed to be familiar with one another. I was still trembling from the adrenaline and I barely registered Martin's hand at the small of my back, supporting me. I turned to him.

"They tried to break into the reference room," I said. Martin's face went white under his beard and his amber eyes widened as he absorbed the news.

"Did they get in? Was anything disturbed or taken?" His voice was pitched higher than normal.

"It looks like the perp was frightened off when I came on the scene with lights and sirens," Tom replied.

"Did the security cameras pick up anything?" Martin asked.

Tom shook his head. "Nothing from inside, just static, which is odd. The exterior cameras did pick up a white car fleeing the scene, though."

I went numb all over. *A white car? Like the car I had been seeing around recently?* Aloud, I said, "It may be just a coincidence, but I've seen a white car, it looks like maybe a Dodge Avenger, sort of following me around the past few days."

Tom immediately whipped out his notebook. "Approximately when and where have you seen this car? Did you get a license plate number or see if it was an out of state plate?"

"No," I said, "I mostly saw the car behind me on the road. I saw it the first time the day I met Martin, and again a couple of times today in town. It was sort of sporty and looked like an older model."

"Any ideas as to who the driver could be?" Tom asked, pen poised above his notepad.

I shook my head helplessly. "No, I have no clue. I didn't even think to mention it to anyone because a sporty white car seems so innocuous. I mean, there are dozens of them in town, let alone the tourists that are around for the festival. I only noticed it because Jed had that Dodge Avenger right out of college, and the driver was super aggressive."

I ran a shaking hand over my face. I felt the barest touch glide over my hair and down my shoulder. I raised my eyes and peered at Martin from under my lashes. He stood innocently gazing at Tom Willis, looking as if butter wouldn't melt in his mouth. *I could have sworn I felt him touch me.*

"Have you seen this white car? Any ideas as to whom it might be?" Tom addressed Martin.

Martin shook his head. "I haven't, but I wasn't the one driving, so I wasn't paying as close attention to the road as Lacey was," he said. "As to who was driving, I have no clue."

Tom flipped his notebook shut and tucked it into his jacket. "Listen, we'll keep an eye out for any white Dodge Avenger type vehicles doing anything suspicious. The library is secure. I checked every nook and cranny, and the intruder is gone. I've already called Jared Baumgartner to come right down and board up the broken window, and I'll wait here until it's installed. I'll escort you inside to survey the damage and see if you can tell if anything is missing."

Guiding me by the elbow, Tom escorted me through the building towards the reference room. He had asked Martin to wait outside. I pressed my hands to my mouth to suppress my gasp of horror as I observed the large, ugly gouges marring the surface of the reference room door.

The narrow window beside the door was covered in a pattern of starred glass in the spots where the perpetrator had smashed something into the glass in an attempt to break it. But the door and the glass had remarkably held. I noticed that the lock had a long metal pick sticking out of it. I assumed that the intruder had tried to pick the lock first, and when that hadn't worked, they had decided to try to brutalize their way in. Other than the vandalism, nothing else looked out of place, and I affirmed that to Tom. I reached for the metal pick, and Tom grasped my forearm.

"Don't touch anything, we'll have to dust for prints once the CSI team arrives from Laketon," he admonished. I pulled my hand back.

"Sorry, I just wanted to do something to try to clean this up," I said helplessly.

Next, Tom led the way to my office. Tears filled my eyes as I took in the broken glass and the shards of pottery and soil from my shattered pothos plant that had been on the shelf under the window. I quickly yanked open my desk drawers and glanced at the contents. I turned to Tom.

"Other than the broken window and my poor plant, everything seems to be here. It seems they just wanted to get into the reference room," I said.

"What's in there that they could possibly want badly enough to break into the library?" Tom asked, clearly puzzled.

I was feeling emotionally raw, and Tom's comment offended me. I squared my shoulders. "There are irreplaceable and important items in there!" I exclaimed. "Maybe *you* don't understand the significance—" I realized abruptly that I was about to throw what my aunt would have called "a major hissy fit" and forced myself to calm down. I took a deep, cleansing breath and released it slowly.

Tom gently reached out and patted my shoulder. "I want you to head home," he said. "There's nothing else for you to do here other than fret." He gave me a stern look from under the brim of his hat. "If you happen to spot that white Dodge Avenger, don't try to engage with the driver, but if there's any way you could discreetly get a license plate or whether it's local or out of state, we'll run the information through our databases and see what we come up with. And even if you can't get those details, let us know immediately if you happen to spot any suspicious cars again."

Tom was a good man, reliable and steady. Janelle was a lucky lady to be attending the Cupid's Ball with him. *You had reliable and steady, and it wasn't enough for you,* my inner critic pointed out. I shrugged it off and thanked Tom, assuring him that I would not try to confront any drivers of white cars any time soon.

We exited the front doors and I saw that Martin was standing next to my car, and he appeared to be staring at his phone. I said good night to Tom, and he headed to his SUV to wait for Jared, the local handyman, to arrive and secure the window.

I dragged myself to my own car and Martin abruptly shoved his phone into his coat pocket.

"Everything okay?" he asked. I didn't trust myself to give details without breaking down, so I merely nodded.

"So, back to the B&B?" I asked him.

"I thought maybe I would take you up on the offer to unpack the papers at your house," he said. He rocked back on his heels and his hands were buried in the pockets of his puffy jacket.

"Well, okay, but we'll have to pick up my daughter first," I replied. I patted my own pockets for my car keys, before I remembered that Martin had driven us to the library.

"I'll need the keys, please. I feel okay driving now." I held out my hand and Martin wordlessly dropped the keys into it without making any contact.

As we settled into the car, I sent a quick text to Jed to let him know that I was on my way over to his place to pick up Claire and we hit the road.

*   *   *

"Wait here, I'll be right back," I told Martin as I pulled up in front of Jed's apartment building. He grunted without looking up from his phone so I jumped out and jogged to the front doors of the building. I buzzed Jed's apartment, and his tinny voice replied that he would be right down. Moments later, the elevator dinged and Jed stepped out holding Claire's hand.

"Hey," he said, his chocolate brown eyes filled with concern. "Is everything okay at the library?"

"Yes, it will be. Someone tried to break into the reference room, but they weren't able to get in. Thank goodness I had extra security put in place last year."

Jed agreed with me, and thanked me for picking up Claire as fast as I was able. He handed me her backpack and to my surprise he followed us out the door.

"I'm on my way to pick up Elaine," he explained after he noticed my look of confusion. "She and I are going for dinner at the El and to see a movie," he continued. Jed's eyes fell to rest on my car, and his eyes narrowed. "Who's that? In your car?" His voice was filled with suspicion.

"Just a friend. He's in town for a family wedding and I'm assisting him with a research project," I replied.

"Hmm, maybe I should meet this guy if he's in your life and you're exposing him to Claire."

"Jed," I sighed, "It's not like that. He's just here for a couple of weeks, he's not going to be 'in my life,' as you put it."

Ignoring me, Jed strode purposefully towards my blue sedan and knocked on the passenger window. I hustled over, hauling Claire by the hand, as Martin lowered the window.

"Hello," Martin said cautiously, eyeballing Jed as he loomed over the car.

"Hi there, Jed Crawford," Jed stuck his hand through the opening. Martin gingerly grasped Jed's hand and shook it as best he could from his awkward seated angle.

"Nice to meet you—Martin Weaver."

Jed's brows went up. "Weaver … are you related to Sheriff Weaver, by any chance?"

"Yes, he's my father. I'm in town for his wedding to Joanna Morton, and I've been working on a project at the library. Lacey here," he inclined his head in my direction, "has been kind enough to spare some time to help me out."

"I see," Jed murmured. Before he could say anything else, my shy and retiring daughter yanked her hand from mine and stepped forward.

"Hi!" she said brightly. "I'm Claire, and I'm almost four years old! What's your name?"

Martin smiled down at her. "My name is Martin, and I'm working with your mom."

Claire's little face scrunched up. "Do you work at the library? I've never seen you there before."

"No, I'm just working on some research at the library, and your mom is helping me out," Martin replied.

"Okay," Claire said, with the complete abrupt acceptance of a small child. She turned back to me. "Can we have breakfast for dinner tonight? Can Martin eat with us?"

I laughed, feeling the stress of the break-in lift for the first time that evening. "Sure, honey. I guess I do owe you some pamcakes, after all."

*   *   *

A short time later, I sat around my dining table in the alcove off the kitchen with Martin and Claire as we polished off the breakfast for dinner that I had prepared.

"That was a wonderful meal," Martin told me, patting his stomach. "Those were some of the best pancakes I've ever had."

"Thanks," I waved him off. "It was just simple pancakes and scrambled eggs. The pancakes are an old family recipe."

"Pamcakes are my favorite!" Claire chimed in.

Martin leaned closer to her and said, "Did you know that in Mexico, they eat the eggs of *bugs* in their pancakes?"

Clarie squealed in either delight or revulsion, it was hard to tell, and shook her head. "No they don't! Mommy, do people eat bug eggs in Mexico?"

I stood and began gathering the empty plates. I arched a brow at Martin and replied, "Actually, yes. They're called ahuautles and they're fried and eaten in pancakes and sometimes tamales. They're also known as Mexican caviar."

"I'm impressed," Martin said over Claire's dramatic "EWWW!"

I tossed my head, my red-gold curls bouncing. "I'm a librarian, babe—prepare to be continually wowed by my vast intellect," I said as I marched into the kitchen with the dinner plates. Martin was hot on my heels.

"Here, let me do that," he said, reaching for the dishes. He slapped on the hot water and pushed in the drain plug.

"You don't have to do that," I started to protest.

"Where's your soap?" he asked, ignoring me. I pointed to the pump dispenser on the corner of the sink and Martin grabbed it and pumped soap into the running water. The bubbles began mounding up immediately as Martin gently slid the plates from my hands and started to ease them into the water. With a shrug, I left him to it and went to get Claire settled and ready for her bath and bed. I reflected that Jed always had to be coerced into dish duty. *Stop comparing him to your ex-husband,* I admonished myself.

When I returned to the living room in my comfy magenta sweatpants and light pink hoodie, Martin had made a pot of tea and was sitting on the couch with two mugs, waiting for me.

"She's a great kid," he said, handing me a steaming mug.

"Thanks, I'm pretty partial to her," I smiled. I tucked my feet underneath me as I settled back and sipped my tea.

"Don't get too comfy, we need to haul in those boxes and get started on them," Martin cautioned me.

"I know, I know. Just give me a few minutes to decompress and digest."

"Dinner, or today's events?" he asked.

"Both," I said, laughing a little. "A lot has happened today."

We sat and sipped in comfortable silence for a few minutes. I was about to ask Martin about his father's wedding plans, when I caught movement out of the corner of my eye. I glanced at the window and clearly saw a pale face peering in. As soon as I focused my gaze, the face vanished. My body went cold and I stiffened and clutched the warm teacup. Martin noticed my reaction.

"Lacey? What's wrong?"

"Don't turn around, but I swear I just saw a face looking in the window," I said through clenched teeth.

Martin immediately turned around and looked. "I don't see anyone," he said as he rose and went to the window to peer out. He pulled the blinds closed, brushed his hands together, and turned back to me.

"Now, where were we?" His voice was filled with forced cheer and I became instantly suspicious.

"Martin, what's going on? I saw your face go practically green at the mention of someone trying to break into the reference room, and that whole white car business." I stood and put my hands on my hips. "And now, you're awfully eager to dismiss me seeing a face in my window. What do you know that you're not telling me?"

Martin threw himself back into the seat he had vacated and leaned back, both hands over his face. He heaved a sigh and pulled his hands down, his fingers stretching his cheeks and hollowing out his eye sockets. Without looking at me, he mumbled, "I think it might be my ex-fiancé."

Chapter Seven

"Ex-fiancé?" I cried shrilly. I dimly recalled that he had previously mentioned buying someone a ring. "Why on earth would your ex-fiancé be outside my window?"

Martin got up from the couch and began pacing back and forth across the worn antique throw rug in shades of yellow and teal. I had never seen him so agitated. He stopped and picked up his mug and frowned at the contents.

"Do you have any Scotch?" he asked me.

"Sorry, English Breakfast is about the strongest drink I've got," I said, shaking my head. Martin set the mug back on the coffee table with a snap.

"She must suspect that I'm on the trail of the missing necklace," he said cryptically as he ran both hands through his wavy auburn hair, clutching the strands and turning it into something resembling a mop.

"Why would she know that? And why would she care about it?" I asked. I pulled the bright pink fuzzy acrylic blanket from the back of the couch and wrapped it around my shoulders, both for warmth and for the feeling of security that it gave me. I burrowed into the blanket and waited for Martin's explanation.

"Her name," he said with a resigned sigh, "is Janine Ellicott."

My jaw dropped as I let out a gasp. "Are you *serious*?" I demanded, then continued without waiting for him to respond. "*The* Janine Ellicott, daughter of the famous billionaire Preston Ellicott?"

Martin nodded miserably, and I kept right on going.

"Janine Ellicott, the gorgeous blonde who was on the cover of *Vogue* twice last year? The same Janine Ellicott who had a cameo as a Bond Girl in the last James Bond film?"

"Yes, yes, *yes!*" Martin snarled, flopping down onto the couch. He clutched one of the patterned throw pillows and then leaned back, covering his face with the pillow.

"Wow," I said, star struck. "I can't believe that *you* were engaged to Janine Ellicott, of all people!"

Martin lowered the pillow and glowered at me.

"You know, I'm not exactly a troll living under a bridge," he snapped.

"Well of course not, I just—I mean—she's like ... a *celebrity*."

"I assure you, she has faults just like any other person."

"Like being an unhinged stalker?" I asked, pulling the blanket closer around my shoulders.

"Her father backed a huge project that I headed up a few years ago, a dig in Mexico." Martin placed the pillow in his lap, and I noticed that his hands were kneading the life out of the poor thing.

"The dig turned up bupkis after six months. Well, bupkis as far as archeological artifacts." He paused and looked at me.

"But …" I prompted.

"But it also turned up evidence that the esteemed Mr. Ellicott was smuggling some very illegal substances from Mexico into the United States."

My jaw fell open. "What?" I asked. I had seen something in the news about Preston Ellicott being under some sort of investigation, and being indicted, but I hadn't paid much attention to the details.

"Now Janine blames me for her father's indictment, and his assets being frozen."

"Why would that be your fault?"

"I was the one who accidentally uncovered the financial discrepancies when I was going over the budgets for the dig. When I brought it up to the wrong people, all the legal troubles started." He jumped up and started pacing again.

I sat and followed him with my eyes as he crossed back and forth across my living room. "I still don't understand why Janine Ellicott would be following you now."

Martin stopped pacing and threw his hands up in the air. "Obviously, she wants to know what we know, and to beat us to the necklace and recoup some of the money I've cost her father. Between the expense of the failed dig, and all the legal fees, and the frozen assets, she's out for both blood and money." Martin's eyes were ablaze.

I was still confused. "But how could she sell the necklace? It's so famous, it would be instantly recognized."

Martin threw back his head and uttered an ugly, sardonic laugh. "Honey, you're pretty naive when it comes to the power of the ultra rich. With her connections, Janine could fence that necklace as easily as you'd hand a peanut butter sandwich to your kid."

"I'm not going to take that as an insult, because I know that you're very upset at the moment," I said primly. "But I think we should call the police."

"The police!" he exploded. "The police would be my father, and I don't need to get him involved in this. Let him enjoy his wedding preparations."

"But I could call Tom—"

"No," Martin said firmly. "I can handle this. My dad is a good sheriff, but these small town cops would be in way over their heads with Janine and the circles she travels in. She won't physically hurt anyone, she's just after the necklace, and my professional reputation, such as it is."

I sat and thought about the situation. My practical side said that I should kick Martin out, drop him and his precious boxes off at the PC B&B and wipe my hands of the whole thing. But another side of me, that side that longed for adventure and romance, insisted that I would be passing up the chance of a lifetime to be involved with finding a historic lost treasure alongside a handsome rogue, like some of my favorite literary characters.

You'll be thirty in a couple of months my inner critic whispered in my ear. I knew in my bones that this was one of those Moments with a capital "M," a crossroads so rarely offered by the fates that allowed me a clear choice of two paths. One path of the same, one path of the unknown.

I drew in a deep breath and looked into Martin's amber eyes and mentally squared my shoulders.

"Then I guess we have no other choice but to find that necklace first. What's our next step?"

Martin crossed the room in two long strides and sat next to me. He wrapped his hands around my shoulders, his golden brown eyes shining.

"Do you mean it?" he asked.

"Yes, let's find that necklace and show this trollop we're not afraid of her!"

Martin's lips twitched. "Did you just use the word 'trollop'?"

I blushed. "It just sort of slipped out."

He finally gave in and laughed his loud and barking laugh that I found so pleasant, and before I knew it, I was laughing too.

"Lacey, I adore you." Martin chuckled. I felt myself go stiff and I abruptly stood up and backed away, letting the blanket tumble into a heap on the floor. Klaxon horns blared in my mind. *This is dangerous territory, tread with caution.*

"Well," I said with false cheer, "let's go get those boxes out of the trunk before the trollop decides to break into my car."

*   *   *

"Shhh!" Martin practically yelled.

I thought it would be prudent to be silent rather than shout about being quiet, but I figured that Martin was nervous. We were skulking along the wall of my house next to the carport, keeping our eyes peeled for Janine. All the lights were off and I shivered and hugged myself in the dim moonlight.

Martin motioned for me to stay put while he crept towards my car. He paused and glanced around furtively before he used the key fob to pop open the old blue sedan's trunk. As he eased the trunk open as slowly as he could, I had to suppress a giggle. Between the tension, and his exaggerated movements, it was almost too much. Martin had insisted on secrecy. He wanted to try and sneak the boxes into my house, in case Janine was nearby spying.

Just as Martin leaned into the trunk, a tall and willowy figure stepped into view at the edge of the carport. In the icy moonlight, I observed a full mane of smooth and shimmering platinum blonde hair that flowed past waist length atop impossibly long legs covered in thigh-high boots with at least four inch heels.

"Hello, Marty," the figure cooed in a deep and sultry voice. Martin startled and his head banged into the lid of the car's trunk as he stood up too quickly. He muttered what sounded like a string of curse words and stood up fully, rubbing the top of his head.

Without taking his eyes off of the woman, Martin said, "Lacey, go inside and lock the door and call the police."

"But I thought you said—"

"Forget what I said, call the police," Martin repeated.

The woman held up her empty hands, palms forward. "I'm not armed, I just want to talk."

"I have nothing to say to you, Janine," Martin crossed his arms defensively across his chest.

"Oh come on, Marty. Just a little chat, for old time's sake?" The woman stepped closer and even in the muted evening light, I could see that she was stunningly gorgeous and at least six feet three inches in those boots. I caught a heavenly whiff of sandalwood and musk wrapped in the mysterious, sensual, and woody base fragrance of the resin oil known as oud. *Probably some ultra haute and wildly expensive designer fragrance,* I thought. I pushed myself away from the wall and took a step towards Martin.

"What do you think—Marty?" I asked him, raising one eyebrow.

"Would everyone *please* stop calling me 'Marty,'" he hissed through clenched teeth. "And as for you," he pointed at Janine, "you're free to move along, and go back to whatever jet-set hole you crawled out of."

Janine took another step forward. "I could buy and sell your hide, Marty, and you know it. My father—"

"Your father is under house arrest!" Martin cut her off.

I stepped in between the former paramours and waved my hands. "Okay, kids, let's all calm down. Maybe we should go inside and talk it through." I was a bit nervous inviting Janine Ellicott into my house, but my instincts said we were safe. I just wanted to drag everything into the light and stop all this sneaking around and spying. "And, I want to know why you broke into my library and caused damage!"

"That's all I'm asking for, just to talk," Janine repeated. "And I have no idea what you're talking about." Janine tossed her shimmering hair and looked defiantly at me.

Martin reluctantly agreed that we should talk and the three of us trooped into my tiny living room. Janine removed her long designer fleece-lined coat and tossed it at me. Feeling like the help, I dutifully hung it on the coat tree next to the door. Janine proceeded to the center of the couch and splayed her long and slinky body gracefully across the piece of furniture, effectively preventing anyone else from sitting there. Jethro and Elly May ran into the room and snuffled at Janine's boots.

"Ugh, I loathe animals, so smelly," Janine shoved the dogs away with one foot. I quickly herded the dogs out to the fenced backyard.

"Would anyone like some tea? Or some hot cocoa?" I asked.

Janine flipped her shining mane of platinum hair over her shoulder. "I'll take a shot of ginger turmeric juice," she said. She looked up from under the fringe of her amazingly plush and long dark lashes. "Organic, of course."

"I'm sorry, I don't have any of that."

"Fine," she waved one long and slender hand that sparkled with several tasteful gold rings, "then I'll have a cold-pressed kale juice."

"I'm afraid I don't have anything but apple juice in the house."

Her enormous pale gray eyes narrowed. "Alright, do you have any alkalized sparkling mineral water?"

"I think I've got a couple of bottles of Topo Chico in the fridge."

Janine sighed. "I suppose that will have to do," she said in a weary tone that implied that she was making quite the sacrifice.

Martin at least had the good grace to look embarrassed. "I'm fine, thank you, Lacey."

I popped into the kitchen and grabbed the bottle of water from the fridge. After a moment's hesitation, I reached into a cabinet for one of the cut crystal glasses from my wedding set and poured the water into it, feeling certain that Janine would balk at drinking directly from the bottle. *Too bourgeois*, I thought. *At least she didn't ask for Cristal champagne.*

I returned to the living room and saw that Martin had taken a seat on the floor, near the coffee table. Janine was still taking up the entire couch, so I took the only seat left, which was a deep blue club chair. I set the bottle of water on a coaster and handed the glass to Janine. She accepted it without thanking me and sipped delicately. Her lush and full lips were slicked with a glossy deep rose color.

"Not bad," she assessed the liquid in her glass. "It could use a twist of Persian lime, but not bad."

Man, I would love to get this woman in the same room as Rayna. My catty thoughts made me smile. Rayna was like the discount store, wanna-be version of Janine. Fascinated, I sat down in the club chair and waited to see what would happen next. Martin looked very uncomfortable, sitting on the floor with a pinched expression on his face.

"Would you like a pillow to sit on?" I asked innocently. "You look uncomfortable."

Martin glared at me, narrowing his brown eyes. "I'm fine, thank you." He turned his attention to Janine. "You wanted to talk, so talk."

I was amused to see that he had slipped a small notebook and pen from his pockets and was prepared to take notes. *Always the scholar,* I thought.

"Why have you been following us in that white car?" I directed the question at Janine.

"I'm sure I don't know what you're talking about, I always drive red cars. They flatter my coloring," she replied.

Janine took a leisurely sip of her sparkling water and swirled the liquid in the glass before she focused on Martin.

"It has come to my attention," she began, "that there are other parties interested in the necklace. The legend is very well known in certain academic and not so academic circles." She set the glass down on the coffee table, ignoring the coaster, and reached for her large leather tote embossed with a fancy logo. She extracted a small leather-bound book faded and covered with stains and cracks.

"I've had people searching for anything related to the McKenna family, and lo and behold, they were able to obtain the personal journal of Maeve Eireen Kelly McKenna." She scanned both of our faces for our reactions. My mouth dropped open and Martin leaped up, banging his knee on the coffee table. He didn't seem to notice.

"What!?" he shouted. "I've been trying to find any sort of personal correspondence or writings from Maeve, and nothing has surfaced so far. I've only found other correspondence *about* her. How did you ..." he trailed off.

"Money, darling. If you offer people enough of it, you'd be surprised at how tirelessly they'll work," Janine said in a smug tone.

"May I?" I held my shaking hand out for the journal. Janine extended it to me, but Martin snatched it out of Janine's hand before I could grasp it.

"Hey!" I said, affronted.

Martin ignored me completely and reverently opened the journal's cracked cover. I was surprised he didn't break out his white cotton gloves.

"I should be wearing gloves," he murmured, as if he had read my mind.

"It hasn't been stored in the best conditions," Janine said. "I believe it was located in a cellar."

Martin studied the pages in front of him, gently leafing through until he found what he was apparently looking for. "The last entry was recorded on February 11, right before she disappeared."

"That makes sense." Turning to Janine, I asked, "Why are you doing this? Why would you give us this information instead of keeping it for yourself?" I threw up my hands. "If you had something this significant, what on earth would you need from the library so badly that you would break in?"

Janine shook her head. "I did no such thing. I'll admit to following you, not that you saw *me*, but only to make sure that the other party wasn't on your tail. As you said yourself, I had the journal. I had no reason to break into your little library."

"Then who—" I began.

"I told you, other parties are after the necklace as well, and they probably assumed that Martin already had the journal and left it in the library," Janine insisted.

I glanced over at Martin, but he was completely absorbed in the contents of the journal, so I focused on Janine. "I still don't understand why you're giving this journal up."

Janine sighed wearily. "Well, honestly, I'm tired of chasing this thing, I just want it found already, and Martin is the best archaeologist I know."

Martin glanced up sharply, and opened his mouth to reply, but Janine continued, "The worst fiancé, but the best archaeologist."

Martin looked offended for a split second, then his face smoothed out. "Touché," he said with resignation. Then his eyes went right back to studying the book in his hands.

"My reputation has taken quite a hit, what with my father's legal troubles and everything," Janine admitted. "If I can be the benefactor who helped find the famous necklace and restore it to its rightful owners, it could go a long way towards repairing the damage."

She drained the glass and set it down. "And Martin is honorable, he'll notify the proper authorities and turn the necklace in. The others searching for it will sell it on the black market and it will be gone forever." She leaned against the cushions and studied her perfectly French-manicured nails. "That would be a shame, especially once you understand what happened to that poor woman," she concluded.

"What happened to her?" I asked, literally on the edge of my seat, all other problems temporarily forgotten. The mystery of the fate of Maeve McKenna had been the stuff of legend around here for nearly a hundred and fifty years.

"She was being stalked," Martin said grimly.

"Stalked?" I was dumbfounded.

"Well, she doesn't specifically refer to it as stalking. The word was in use in the fifteenth century as a term for one who hunts, but the term wasn't used to indicate obsessive harassment until the early 1990s."

"Thanks for the history lesson, professor," I snarked.

"Anyway, she writes about how her husband knew nothing about this person—she never mentions his name, merely refers to him as 'JP'—and it seems that it was someone she knew from when she lived in her home country," Martin continued. "But he followed her and was constantly threatening her." He held up the journal.

"According to the passages I've read so far," he said, "he would make threats to harm her children if she ever revealed his harassment to her husband or to the authorities. Not that anyone would believe in those days that a woman could be in danger from a stalker." He shook his head in disgust. "The meager anti-stalking laws we do have didn't come about until the late 20th century."

"Maeve would also lock herself in her rooms for weeks at a time, telling the servants that she was suffering another bout of melancholia from being homesick," Janine added. "She was hoping that if she stayed out of sight for long enough, this JP would give up and go home. I've read that journal from cover to cover, and believe me, she was desperate to escape this JP person."

"Did he kill her and then cover it up?" I asked, horrified.

"Not according to her journal," Janine replied. "You understand that back in those days, she wouldn't have been able to escape easily. A woman was under the authority of her husband, all property and money belonged to him, and the wife would have very little resources in the way of financial assistance or protection."

"That's unfortunately all too true," I acknowledged. "But she disappeared, so what happened? Did she find a way to get out? Maybe she sold the necklace and used the money to fund a new life."

Janine poured the rest of the bottle of sparkling water into the emptied glass and took a sip before she answered my questions.

"You've heard about the man seen lurking on the grounds of the McKenna mansion prior to her disappearance?" she asked.

I nodded impatiently and gestured for her to continue.

"Well, that man was none other than JP, that she knew from the old country, and apparently she offered to give him the necklace as payment for letting her go, and leaving her children alone," Janine said.

"So, he had the necklace?" I asked.

Janine shook her head, her shining platinum hair swaying like a silky curtain. "You would think so, but the deal was that she was to get the necklace out of the safe, and hide it in an assigned spot for JP to find, and Maeve would disclose that hiding spot once she was safely on a ship bound for another country." She paused for a breath.

"I sense a 'but' coming on," I interjected.

"But," Janine said, "we have no way of knowing if JP retrieved the necklace. It was never seen again. Maeve ran for her life, the last entry is clear on that, but the necklace was already hidden and she had no time to retrieve it if the timeline is correct."

"What does the last entry say?" I looked at Martin.

He leafed through the book and stopped when he found the page and began to read aloud in his clear lecturer's voice.

"'February 11. This is my last hope to save myself and my husband and children. I must flee this place tonight, before JP returns, lest he changes his mind about the necklace and comes after me once more. My heart is torn in two at the thought of leaving my sons, but JP has threatened them one too many times and they will undoubtedly be safer in my absence, and Nanny Primm will take good care of them. I can only imagine what people will say about me after I am gone. I sincerely hope that my husband will find it in his heart to forgive me someday, as it is also for his safety that I must leave, for JP has many times intimated that if I were no longer married he could claim me for his own. It would be simpler if I loved JP and wanted to run away with him, but he is a cruel and frightening man. My only chance is to leave immediately with the clothes on my back and seek a new fortune elsewhere. I had intended to burn this journal, but I cannot bear the thought of no one ever knowing what became of me, why I had to flee, and so in the event that this may bring my fate to light some day, I will hide it well and hope that someday it may be found. I must go now, I have booked passage under the name Julia Flaherty, and the ship leaves tonight. I am terrified that JP will follow, but if he does, at least I shall draw him away from my family. Pray for me.'"

Martin closed the book and looked at each of us in turn.

"So we know she ran, and why, but we don't know where she ended up." Martin shook his head. "This journal almost gives us more questions than answers at this point." He put the book on the coffee table and started his pacing routine again. "I'll need to search the ship's manifest around that time for anyone by that name …"

"I have to wonder why she suddenly made plans to escape, especially without her boys, after suffering through it for years," I mused. "Was there a catalyst that inspired her to get out?"

Janine shrugged and drained her glass for the second time. "JP was harassing her to leave and be with him, but Maeve says that she couldn't bear the scandal that it would bring to her husband and children, and she did come to love Merrick, at least a little bit. JP started resorting to threatening to do away with Merrick and the children because he saw them as an impediment to having Maeve with him."

"I still don't see why she didn't tell the police—" I began.

"The police and everyone else would have more than likely accused Maeve of bringing the unwanted attention onto herself," Martin said. "You're thinking like a 21st century woman with 21st century rights and protections. Those rights and protections didn't exist back then," he reminded me.

"Maybe the papers from Bill Hanrahan's family will have some clue as to what happened to her," I said to Martin.

"We'd better get them out of the trunk into the house, bugs or no bugs," he replied.

"Bugs?" Janine's lip curled in revulsion.

"We?" I looked just as horrified. "What if the clowns who broke into the library get the bright idea to come looking here?" My voice became louder and more shrill as I continued to rant. "I have a kid! I won't risk her safety!"

"Mommy?" Claire stood at the entrance to the hallway in her flannel nightgown, her Elsa doll dangling from one hand, rubbing her eyes. "Why is everybody yelling?"

"Oh, honey, we woke you!" I hurried over to my daughter and scooped her up into my arms. "I'm sorry, baby, everything is okay. We were just talking." I buried my face in her blonde hair and inhaled the scent of strawberry baby shampoo before planting a kiss on the top of her head and setting her back on her feet.

Claire's gaze traveled around the room and stopped on Janine. She crossed the room and stood right in front of the glamorous woman and studied her with wide eyes.

"You're pretty. You look like Elsa," she said reverently.

Janine smiled, and her face went from beautiful to traffic-stopping gorgeous. "Why thank you! You're very pretty, too. I like your curls. What's your name? I'm Janine." She patted the couch next to her and Claire climbed right up and sat down.

"My name is Claire. I'm almost four. How old are you?"

Martin choked and started to cough violently. I pounded on his back between his shoulder blades and waited to see what Janine would say.

"Oh, I'm old enough to know better," she told Claire with a grin. Claire reached out and stroked Janine's long blonde locks where they flowed down over her shoulder.

"Is your hair real?" she asked.

Uh oh, I need to interject before things get more awkward.

"Claire, honey, you should go back to bed. Why don't I make you some warm milk, and you can drink it in your room?" This was an offer she wouldn't be able to refuse, since I usually had a strict policy forbidding any food or beverages in her room. As predicted, her eyes lit up.

"I can have milk in my room?"

"Yes, if you go right now, I'll bring it to you," I told her. She slid off the couch and pounded down the hall at a dead run for her room.

As I headed for the kitchen to get the warm milk, Janine rose from the couch.

"I had better go. I suggest that you get those documents you obtained today to a safe place and go through them as soon as possible." She went to the front door and stood near the coat rack. I didn't know what she was doing just standing there, so I watched from the kitchen doorway until Martin heaved a sigh and grabbed her coat from the rack and held it out for her to slide into.

"Thank you, Janine," he said grudgingly, "even if I still think you're doing this for less than altruistic reasons, I'm grateful for the incredible lead you've given me." With a courtly little bow, he opened the front door for her, and Janine winked at me over her shoulder.

"Bye, Lindy!" she called and then she stalked gracefully out of the house and into the frigid January night.

"It's Lacey," I murmured to no one in particular.

Martin turned to me, concern etched on his face. "I don't think you should be here alone with Claire as long as those boxes are on your property," he said.

"I agree," I replied. Martin's eyebrows disappeared under his shaggy mop of chestnut colored bangs and his eyes widened.

"Oh relax, Casanova, you'll be sleeping on the couch," I told him, picking up my magenta blanket and tossing it at him. He reached out and caught the blanket instinctively and then looked down at it with distaste. He glanced up at me and hastily smoothed his features out.

"Of course! Looks nice and warm," he said, clutching the blanket to his chest.

"I'll get Claire her milk, and get a spare pillow for you, and we can have a talk and come up with a plan."

"Good idea. In the meantime, I think we should get the boxes secured in the house. They're too vulnerable out there in the trunk of your car," Martin said over his shoulder as he moved to the front door.

"Okay." I watched him walk through the door, his slim silhouette illuminated by the porch light. As he closed the door behind him, I turned and went to the kitchen to heat up some milk in Claire's favorite unicorn mug. After settling my daughter, I stepped into my bedroom to grab a spare pillow.

With a jolt, I realized that this had been Jed's pillow before he had moved out. I shook it off, telling myself to stop being so sentimental. It was just a pillow, for goodness sake, and an inanimate object. It had been washed and dried dozens of times since Jed had last used it. I quickly changed out the pillowcase for a fresh one and carried the pillow back to the living room just as Martin was coming in with the last of the boxes.

He had stacked the boxes in the corner behind the dining room table, away from any windows. As he set the final box atop the others, his hands lingered over the cardboard flaps and I could see that he was itching to get into the contents. Reluctantly, he stepped away from the cartons. "I guess we'd better hope these are bug-free," he said in a wry tone.

I shuddered. "It's getting late, let's get a plan together so we can both try and get some sleep," I said, stifling a yawn.

In reply, Martin whipped out his ever-present notebook and settled at the table, beckoning me to join him.

Chapter Eight

I pulled into the parking lot of the library at seven the next morning, bleary-eyed and exhausted. I had been up into the small hours of the morning, talking over the journal and the issue of what to do with the boxes of documents from Bill Hanrahan. We had ultimately decided that Martin should take the boxes and Maeve's journal to the sheriff's department, and ask his father to store them in the evidence lockup.

Martin vowed to make a big show of loading the boxes into the sheriff's cruiser, in case anyone was watching. He would do a run-through of the boxes and sort the contents preliminarily. I planned to make a copy of the journal on the printer at the library.

I patted my purse, feeling the little book contained inside before I hauled myself out of the car. It gave me a thrill to touch and hold the old book, caressing the worn and cracked leather, and to feel a direct connection to history through the living handwriting of a woman whose bones were now dust.

My mind kept wandering back to waking up this morning, stumbling out to the kitchen to get the coffee going, and seeing Martin's form curled up on the couch, an indiscriminate lump under the fuzzy hot pink blanket with Elly May curled up behind his knees.

When I had walked in to wake him, he sat up and displayed a very fine lean and muscular torso. I had released an involuntary gasp of delight that I covered by pretending to have a coughing fit.

We had shared a quick cup of coffee and some toast together before he called his father, and I departed for the preschool to drop off Claire on my way to work. I had forgotten how nice it was to share a moment in the morning with someone like that. Touching base, sharing how well you did or didn't sleep, sharing your plans and goals for the day. Martin had even made a joke about my frizzy bed-head morning hair. I caught myself wearing a goofy grin in the reflection of the car window, despite being so tired that I felt like I could drop at any moment.

A battered tan pickup truck with a camper shell turned into the lot. "Baumgartner's Handyman Services" was hand-painted on the side in faded black lettering over a phone number. Jared Baumgartner was a great-nephew to the longtime principal of Pinewood High School, Mary Baumgartner. The truck pulled into the space next to me, and a stout man in worn jeans, work boots, and a thick down vest over a plaid shirt, sporting a head of dark blond hair styled in a bowl cut and a longish beard, got out and waved.

"Good morning, Jared," I greeted him.

"Morning, Lacey," he replied. "I'm here to take measurements on your office window, and the window next to the reference room, so that I can order the replacement glass." He paused for a moment and looked thoughtful. "Of course, the glass from the reference room is reinforced glass, and it will take a bit longer to get ahold of."

"That's fine, Jared," I assured him. "I'm glad you're here." I grimaced at the thought of the cost, though. The library was operating on a shoe-string budget as it was.

"I used my shop vac and cleaned up the glass and put up plywood last night," Jared informed me.

We crossed the parking lot together, and I was dismayed to see another car enter the library's parking lot. This car was a bright red Lexus, and it belonged to none other than Rayna Reese. *She'll want to interview me about the break-in,* I realized. I would have no choice but to speak to her and try to give the facts, if I didn't want some lurid exaggeration published.

Steeling myself for impact, I opened the doors, disabled the alarm, and went inside with Jared following behind. I waved him off to do what he needed to do while I completed my opening tasks and waited for Rayna to enter the building.

*   *   *

The interview was fairly painless. I gave Rayna the facts and she sounded almost sincere when she told me that she was glad that I wasn't harmed. I felt confident that the article would be a good account of what had actually happened.

The library was unusually busy, with many patrons looking to indulge in gossip about the break in, and I was actually relieved to be able to tell them that they could read all about it in tomorrow's edition of the Pinewood Courier.

By the time closing rolled around, I was exhausted. I gave Miriam a grateful wave goodbye as she shrugged into her coat and left, silver braids swinging as she made her way out the doors. I was about to lock the doors when the phone on the checkout desk began to ring. I grabbed the receiver.

"Pinewood Corners Public Library, Lacey speaking, how can I help you?"

"Hi Lacey, it's Jared. I wanted to let you know that I'll be back the day after tomorrow to install the glass in your office window. The reinforced glass will take a few more days to come in."

I felt a tension headache coming on and I pinched the bridge of my nose. "Please make sure that you get the invoice estimates for me as soon as possible so that I can get started on filing the insurance claim."

"No need for that. Some lady called me, her name was Joleen or something, said to send the bill to her and she would take care of it. Said you had enough on your plate," Jared replied.

"Do you mean Janine?" I asked, my voice rising with shock.

"Yeah, could be. Anyway, nice lady. I'll see you the day after tomorrow." Jared hung up and I stood there stunned, holding the dead receiver against my ear. *Janine had paid for all the repairs to the library?* Just as I finally placed the phone into its cradle, my cell phone buzzed in my pocket. I pulled it out and glanced at the screen. It was Martin. Absurdly pleased, I swiped the green answer button.

"Hey, there, Indiana Jones," I greeted him. "How goes the preliminary search of the boxes?"

"Indiana Jones is a terrible archeologist. He never maps or measures anything, he never files any forms with the historic preservation office, he never photographs or documents any artifacts in situ, he just grabs and runs like a common thief—"

"Okay, okay, I get it," I interrupted his tirade. "We were busy at the library today, but I managed to get the journal pages copied."

"Excellent. How about you swing by the municipal building and pick me up? We can grab something to eat and I'll tell you about what I've discovered so far."

"It's a deal," I replied, and I couldn't keep the smile out of my voice.

*   *   *

When I pulled into the lot of the Wingate County Municipal complex, the sun had nearly set, robbing what little color there was from the winter landscape. The original main building dated back to the early days of the town, and it boasted intricate masonry and mullioned windows. The main building housed the mayor's offices and the town council and historical society. The sheriff's office and county jail were in a newer building that was separate but adjacent, as was the courthouse.

I texted Martin that I had arrived, and I saw the unmistakable silhouette of his slender form exit the double doors of the sheriff's office. His head swiveled as he scanned the parking lot, and his hand went up in a wave of acknowledgement when he spotted my car. I was surprised at the sensation of butterflies in my stomach as he approached the car.

It's nothing, it's only the anticipation of learning about what he's found in those boxes, not anything to do with him, I told myself. *Because it's fine to be excited about things, because things are simple and concrete. People aren't. People have complicated minds and agendas of their own, they leave, they disappear, and even if they stay, the feelings disappear.*

Martin strolled up to the driver's side window. I lowered it and Claire's voice piped up from the backseat.

"Hi, Mister Martin!" In her excitement, she started kicking the back of my seat.

"Hi, there, Miss Claire!" Martin replied with a little wave, leaning into the window.

Claire giggled. "You made a rhyme," she cried, obviously delighted. "Are you coming over for pamcakes again?" she asked him.

Martin's eyes met mine, and he said, "As delicious as your mom's pamcakes are, I think she's had a very long day. If it's okay with you, I thought we might order a pizza."

"Yay, pizza!" Claire cheered. "I want perponi."

"It's *pepperoni*, honey, and we can definitely make that happen," I said, laughing. I knew that it would be all too soon when Claire would be too big to make those cute little blunders, and I also knew that I would miss them dearly.

"But first," Martin said, putting out his hand, "I'll take that journal to the lockup."

"Of course!" I reached into my purse and pulled out the journal. My fingers were reluctant to let the little book go, though, and I gripped it tightly for a moment before releasing it into Martin's gloved hands. His eyes met mine again, and a spark of understanding arose, as if to say *I know, it's amazing, isn't it?*

"Be right back," he said over his shoulder as he trotted towards the warm glow of light shining from the front doors of the building in the growing darkness. I raised the window up and shivered. I turned the car's heater up a couple of degrees and waited for Martin to return.

"Mommy, can we listen to music?" Claire asked.

"Sure, baby. What should we put on?" I responded, steeling myself for the ten thousandth play of the *Frozen* soundtrack.

To my surprise, she asked for "Shake It Off" by Taylor Swift. I pulled up the song from my *Legendary Ladies* playlist, and by the time Martin returned, Claire and I were both singing along to the spunky lyrics.

Martin scowled in the gleam of the overhead dome light as he climbed into the passenger seat. I looked directly at him and shouted out the words playing over the speakers, and I shimmied my shoulders for extra emphasis. Martin's scowl morphed into a rueful grin. To his credit, he stayed silent until the song ended. I hit the pause button. Claire cried out in protest.

"Hush now, Mister Martin and I need to talk for a minute," I told her, glancing at her pouting face in the rearview mirror. I reached for a bag of goldfish crackers from the console, tore it open, and handed it to her over the seat. "Here's a little snack to tide you over until dinner," I said. Claire practically snatched the bag out of my hands. *Her blood sugar must be low,* I thought, as I said aloud, "What do you say?"

"Thank you, Mommy," she mumbled through a mouthful of crackers.

"Don't talk with your mouth full," I automatically said.

"Sorry," Claire replied, her voice muffled by crackers. I mentally rolled my eyes and let it go, turning to Martin.

"So did we want take-out, delivery, or dine in? Martinelli's offers all three options," I said.

"Let's do take-out, that way we can settle in and talk privately," Martin replied, settling into his seat.

"You've got it," I put the car in gear and cruised through the parking lot towards the road. Main Street was crowded with traffic and pedestrians.

"It looks like the festival traffic is starting," I remarked.

"What day is it?" Martin sounded genuinely confused.

"The 31st, the Sweetheart Soiree festival officially starts tomorrow," I replied.

Martin rubbed his hands over his eyes. "I've been so focused on this project, I forgot what the date is." Out of the corner of my eye, I could see him looking at me speculatively. As I rolled to a stop at an intersection, I glanced over at him.

"What?" I asked.

"What are you doing tomorrow?"

"Well, we're supposed to meet Joanna Morten at her house for breakfast and then I have my shift at the library." I drove through the intersection, grateful that the traffic thinned at this end of Main Street, and then reached to flip my signal to turn into the parking lot of Martinelli's Pizza, Wings and Things. Suddenly, Martin gripped my elbow. His hold was firm and warm.

"Keep going," he hissed, his voice tight with urgency. "Don't turn in here, just keep on going straight."

"Why? I thought—"

"Just do it," he said in a quiet but firm tone. I could see him pulling his phone from his pocket. "Dad? I see the white car again. We're heading north on Main, just past Oak."

I felt as if a giant, icy vice grip had suddenly squeezed my entire body as I went numb with cold fear. I glanced in the rearview mirror, spotting a pair of headlights a couple of car lengths back. I also saw my little girl in the backseat, happily munching on cheddar crackers, not a care in the world. My heart lurched and I stepped hard on the gas pedal.

"Lacey," Martin's voice was calm and steady. "Just go at the normal speed, don't let on that you're aware of them. Tom's been dispatched, he'll find us."

My knuckles were dead white from gripping the wheel, and my shoulders were just about buried in my ears.

"It's okay, Lacey. We're safe, just breathe. Slow and steady, breathe in, nice and deep … let it out. That's good," Martin's voice was calm and steady, and I clung to it like a life preserver in a stormy sea. After being guided through a few breaths, I felt calmer and more in control.

"Thanks," I said on one of my exhales. Martin patted me on the shoulder. Just as I was feeling calmer, the car's interior lit up with pulsing red and blue light as the unmistakable shriek of a police siren tore through the night. I gasped and returned immediately to clutching the wheel and hyperventilating.

A streak of white slingshotted past us in the right lane, going so fast that it was a blur, followed by a Wingate County Sheriff's SUV, lights and sirens in full effect as it pursued the mysterious white car. Shaking, I popped my signal on and pulled into the first parking lot I came across. As I guided the car in between the lines of an empty spot, I put the car into park with trembling hands.

"Mommy, are we buying shampoo and toothpaste?" Claire asked. I glanced up and realized that we were in the parking lot of Marcus Pharmacy. "Can we go inside and say hi to Miss Elaine?" I had forgotten that Jed's new girlfriend worked here as a pharmacy technician.

"Mommy just needs a minute, honey," I told her, trying to sound reassuring. I took my phone from its mount on the dash and pulled up the YouTube app and opened the kids version. I handed the phone into Claire's eager hands. She would be happily occupied for a little while at least, since I rarely utilized the electronic babysitter. I concentrated on taking deep breaths as Martin sat quietly, typing on his phone. He glanced up at me.

"You did great, Lacey."

After some time had passed, his phone rang. He answered and I heard his soft murmurs of things like "Okay, mmm-hmm, yes, thank you." He ended the call.

"Tom chased the car all the way to the edge of town before he lost them on Ridge Road. He got the plates, though. The car is registered to a company, BBR, LLC. The company doesn't seem to have a website or an EIN, so it's probably some sort of a shadow corporation. Tom is on his way back, and he or another officer will be keeping an eye on you and Claire until these people are apprehended."

I covered my face with my hands and drew in another deep, shaky breath. "Okay, what do we do now?" My words were muffled by my palms. Instead of a direct answer, I heard Martin speaking into his phone again.

"Hi, I'd like to order a large pepperoni pizza, an order of medium-spicy wings, and-do you have garlic knots? Okay, some cheesy garlic breadsticks, then." I glanced over at him in the dim yellow light of the pharmacy sign and he raised his brows and mouthed *anything else?* I shook my head and he spoke aloud again. "Yes, that will do it, to go please, we'll pick it up shortly, thank you." He hung up with a satisfied smile.

"So," I said, "I guess we resume our earlier plans, then?"

"Sure, might as well," Martin replied. "The imminent danger is gone, and I'm hungry, and I'm sure you and Claire are, too."

"Perponi pizza!" Claire cheered from the back seat.

*   *   *

Soon, we were settled at my dining room table, munching on slices of pizza and passing around the breadsticks, which Claire loved. She made a face over the wings, though, and refused to try them.

"More for me, then," Martin said with a wink. He ate the wings by inserting the entire piece of meat into his mouth and pulling on the bone, stripping off the edible portion in one sweep.

"They're all yours," I told him. I personally didn't care for wings—too much work to get a tiny bit of meat off the bone. And the thought of eating skin made me cringe.

After we had stuffed ourselves, I got Claire settled in the living room with a scoop of vanilla ice cream and yet another screening of *Frozen*. Martin and I settled at the now-cleared kitchen table to talk.

"Thanks," he said as I handed over the folder that contained the copied pages of the journal. "I got through all the boxes from Mr. Hanrahan, and I was able to separate the contents out into useful, maybe useful, and junk."

"Old greeting cards and expired coupons?" I couldn't resist teasing him.

"Pretty much," he said with a chuckle, "along with a bunch of recipes clipped from magazines and a handful of warranties for appliances purchased in the 1970s." Martin took a swig from the can of soda on the table at his elbow. "But there were some treasures mixed in with the trash." He leaned back slightly and crossed his arms, his light brown eyes dancing.

I could tell that he was enjoying this, dragging out his discoveries and baiting my curiosity. I played along.

"Treasures? You're killing me over here. Spill! What sort of treasures? A bunch of dog hair, probably. Not the necklace, surely?" I raised one eyebrow.

Martin laughed his hearty and pleasant laugh, and I grinned.

"No, unfortunately, I did not come across a half a million dollar necklace buried in the cartons of a lonely old man." He paused again for effect, his eyes slanted towards me, and I realized what a superb lecturer he must be.

"I found another journal, and some letters tied with ribbon that are from the time period in question. They are addressed to M.E. O'Grady, which fits with the Hanrahan's family maid at the time."

"Why would the Hanrahans have kept her things mixed in with theirs?" I asked.

"She worked for the family for most of her life, even had a daughter that lived in her quarters with her that she raised along with the Hanrahan children." Martin absently reached for his soda again. "They must have thought of her as family."

"Why didn't the daughter take possession of her mother's things, I wonder?"

Martin's shoulders bobbed up and down. "We may never know, but maybe there will be something in the journal or papers that will indicate a reason why."

I tapped my fingers in a staccato beat on the table top, a habit I developed while thinking. "I wish we had the stuff here, to read over tonight," I lamented.

"You know why we can't do that," Martin's eyes traveled to where Claire sat in the next room.

"I do," I replied. Without warning, Martin's calloused hand closed over mine, stopping the beat of my fingers. My traitorous heartbeat sped up as a tingle shot all the way up my arm at his touch.

"Listen, what time does your shift end at the library tomorrow?" he asked.

Startled at the sudden change of subject, I replied, "Four, why?"

"I thought maybe you and Claire and I should partake in some of the opening day activities of the festival," he said.

"Do you think we really have the time to spare on such a frivolous—" I began. Martin stopped my words with a slight shake of his shaggy head.

"Prolonged tension leads to poor results," he said. "We should relax a little, do something fun to take our minds off of the situation."

"Is that safe, all things considered?" I asked, my green eyes wide with worry.

"It's safer for us to be in public, in a crowded space surrounded by people," he said, giving my hand a reassuring squeeze before he released it.

"Where are you spending the day tomorrow?" I asked. "After we meet for breakfast, I mean."

"I was going to catch a ride in the morning with my dad to Jo's house for breakfast, and then he'll take me back to the sheriff's station. I'll spend the day poring over the journal and the packs of letters."

"Okay, after I'm off work, I'll pick up Claire at the pre-school and then swing by the station to pick you up, and we'll see what the festival has to offer."

Chapter Nine

I rolled over again and punched my flattened pillow to fluff it up under my head. I had been tossing and turning since Martin left. We had stood in the doorway, and Martin gave me a friendly pat on the shoulder and told me that he would see me in the morning. Then he called his father to drive him back to the B&B. I felt vaguely disappointed and incomplete somehow.

What had I expected, really? We'd only been hanging out for a few days, and he'll be leaving in a couple of weeks. Besides, he's so scholarly, and he doesn't like music or movies or TV or … I flipped over again with a huff. *He's also gallant, intelligent, passionate about history and research, he likes Claire, and she likes him, he smells great …*

Giving up on sleep for the time being, I reached up and flipped on my bedside lamp. Squinting in the sudden brilliance of the sixty watt bulb, I fumbled on the night table for my trusty journal. For me, there was nothing better for getting out my thoughts and anxieties than by journaling. My journal never judged, never tried to give unwanted advice—my journal just patiently listened to my cares and worries and eased my mind. The little book felt comforting in my hands. I took the pen from its elastic loop and opened the journal.

I can't sleep. Why can't I get Martin out of my head? He's so different from any man I've known. Sure, there were some guys in college that were really dry and scholarly, but I was never attracted to them. I was married back then.

Sometimes it feels like I'm living my life backwards—married before college, becoming a mom, and now single and attracted to a man other than Jed for the first time. Attracted to the first man ever, really.

My teenage hormones had barely begun to blossom when Jed asked me out after we'd been hanging out for a few years. I've never really gone on a date in the conventional sense of the word, a date where you get together with someone you're romantically interested in, to spend some time with them, get to know them better, learn their likes and dislikes. I knew Jed so well by the time we morphed our friendship into a romantic relationship, we didn't need that "getting to know you" phase. We basically grew up together. Up and apart, eventually.

Now I don't have any idea what I'm doing, and I can't read Martin. How does he feel about me? And does it even matter? He's leaving for Mexico after Valentine's Day. Mexico swallows people up, never to be seen again.

He leads the life of a nomad, and I have my dream job at the library, and Claire needs stability. It wouldn't be possible to go gallivanting around with him, even if he invited us. Why am I even allowing myself to enter-tain that idea? I'm a small-town librarian and proud of it. I don't want to change myself into some jet-set vagabond.

Speaking of, Martin dates billionaire supermodels. Well, only one billionaire supermodel, to be fair. But most people don't get to be involved with even one, so that's technically a lot. How could I possibly even com-pare? I'm fooling myself. I'm sure he's enjoying my company as a "sound-ing board" and a ride around town, nothing more. I'm probably reading into things, simply because I've been feeling lonely. That's no reason to go nuts over the first man to stumble into my path. Best to tamp down these thoughts and feelings and keep my heart and my life safe. It's only two weeks.

I don't want to stop spending time with Martin, though—I'm in this necklace business up to my ears, and I'm invested in seeing how this turns out. Even though it's frightening to have the mysterious white car following us, and unknown parties breaking into the library, the prospect of solving the town's biggest mystery is irresistible. And really, other than the damage to the library, there's been no physical threats or harm.

Plus, I'll admit that the research side of things, and the pull of his-tory are very satisfying. I wanted some adventure and intrigue and now I've got it. I wanted some romance, too, but honestly, the idea of melding a stranger's life with my established and comfortable life scares me even more than being tailed by nefarious characters while searching for a price-less piece of jewelry.

We're going to the festival tomorrow evening, and I'm sure that's just Martin being friendly and trying to pay me back for driving him hither and yon for the past few days. I just need to friend-zone Martin and hang in there until Valentine's Day. It will arrive before I know it, and then things can go back to normal around here.

I closed the book. Journaling had worked its magic and my eyelids were now heavy, my body relaxed. As I finally drifted into sleep, my last thoughts were of Martin's unusual golden brown eyes surrounded by a thick brush of lashes, and his contagious laughter.

*   *   *

I was running late, again. It was ten minutes after seven when I pulled into Joanna Morten's driveway. I started to park behind Sheriff Weaver's patrol car, but thought the better of it. What if he was called out suddenly on some sort of emergency? I backed out of the driveway and parked along the curb instead. As I rushed up the path to the side door, picking my way around patches of snow on the ground, I smiled at the big plastic hearts and the flamingos wearing heart-shaped sunglasses stuck in the partially frozen ground, peppering Jo's front yard.

I rapped twice on the glass of the storm door before opening it and letting myself in, as was my habit whenever I visited. The air was redolent with the homey smells of coffee, bacon and freshly baked biscuits. As I was removing my boots, I heard Jo's cheerful voice call out from the back of the house.

"We're in the kitchen, come on back!"

I entered the sunny yellow and blue kitchen and felt my shoulders relax completely for the first time in days. I had spent many an hour in this kitchen, conferring with my best friend Mikki, eating cookies and drinking tea and hot chocolate in the winter and iced tea and strawberry lemonade in the summer.

"Morning, everyone!" I said with a wave. I saw that Jo, her fiancé, and Martin were all seated at the round table tucked into the nook created by the bay window. I tried not to let my gaze linger too long on Martin. His hair was combed neatly back for once, and he was dressed in a red and black buffalo plaid shirt that flattered his auburn beard.

"Hey, Lacey." The sheriff gallantly stood, and Martin quickly followed.

"Morning." Martin pulled out the last empty chair for me and I awkwardly sat, smoothing my pencil skirt, and hitched myself forward as the chair was pushed in. I was not used to this kind of treatment, but I hoped it didn't show. Martin's hand brushed across my shoulders as he stepped away, and I shivered.

"Oh, my dear, are you cold?" Jo leaned forward, concerned. "Here, have some coffee, that will warm you right up." She poured coffee into my cup from an insulated carafe on the table. I thanked her and added cream and sugar, grateful for having something to occupy my attention while Martin and his father resumed their seats.

"Help yourself, we've already started." Jo gestured at the platters of fluffy scrambled eggs, crisp bacon and a mountain of biscuits. I saw butter along with various containers of jams and honey. My mouth watered.

"Thanks. I love your biscuits!" I split and buttered a tall biscuit and slathered on strawberry jam before greedily stuffing half of it in my mouth.

Jo laughed, bringing a pretty flush to her cheeks that complimented her bright red sweater covered in little white hearts.

"I love to see you enjoy, dear," she said, her blue eyes sparkling. I nodded, my mouth full of biscuit. As soon as I swallowed, I asked her about Mikki's whereabouts.

"I didn't see her car outside, I figure she's at the new bakery," I said.

"Yes, she and Michael have been working day and night to get everything ready for the grand opening today. I heard her leave the house around four this morning. I'm so proud of her and Michael, they've worked so hard and I just know that their bakery is going to be a success. It's got too much love put into it to fail."

"Lacey and I are taking in the festival tonight with Claire. We'll have to stop in at the bakery," Martin interjected.

"We were just talking about the case," Sheriff Weaver said. "Jo and I grew up with the legend as well, although the events surrounding Mrs. McKenna and the necklace were only about eighty years in the past when Jo and I were born." He reached across the table and gave Jo's hand an affectionate squeeze.

"Yes, my family had ties to the McKennas," Jo said. "A few of my ancestors even worked for them back in the day."

"Really?" I was intrigued. "Did they ever talk to you about it?"

"Oh, they were long gone by the time I was a girl," she said. "Maeve's sons had grown up and the younger one married into the Reese family—they were always influential around these parts, and the Reese women were known for their beauty, even back then." Her eyes clouded over as she gazed into the past. "Of course, there were rumors of a curse—silly, really—because the McKenna fortunes steadily declined after Maeve disappeared, and one of the McKenna boys never had children—he was the one who married a Reese girl, so the Reese family today doesn't have any blood ties to the McKennas. The other had plenty of children, but most of them didn't make it past their fifth birthday."

I cried out involuntarily. "That's terrible!"

Jo shook her head, frowning. "That's just how it was back then. No antibiotics and plenty of fevers and flus other diseases that hit children the hardest. One of them, a son, survived to adulthood. He was born around 1885, I think."

I heard a scrabbling sound and glanced over at Martin. He was taking notes. *Of course!*

"Do you know the son's name?" he asked.

"Robert? Albert? Herbert? Something like that. It's been a while since I left the historical society," Jo replied.

"Why did you? Leave, I mean," Martin asked her.

"Because I was tired of dealing with those stuffy old prigs," she said indignantly. "They said I wasn't, and I quote, 'historical society material' because, according to them, I dressed too crudely and they said I was tacky." She crossed her arms, eyes flashing almost as fiercely as the light-up earrings she wore, a white cupid in her right ear and a red glittering arrow pulsing brightly in her left. "Tacky!" she harrumphed.

"What ever happened to Robert-Albert-Herbert?" Martin asked, pen poised over his notes.

"Oh, he had a couple of daughters. By then, the McKenna family coffers were just about empty. The grand mansion was abandoned, with no money for upkeep. It's now the town museum and convention center. They hold the Cupid's Ball and things like that there, and they turned Merrick McKenna's original mercantile store into the post office. Anyway, the daughters were born between 1910 and 1915 or so, and they eventually grew up and married and had a few children of their own."

She paused for a sip of coffee before she continued. "If memory serves, the older daughter had one boy, born around 1940, and he was killed as a young man in the Vietnam War without ever having any children. The younger daughter had two girls, born in the 1940s, and one died relatively young without ever marrying or having children, and the other had one son who died in the 1980s, also without children." Jo set her coffee cup on the table with a definitive thunk. "And that was the end of the direct line of the McKenna family."

"What do you know about the Hanrahans?" I asked as I helped myself to several slices of bacon.

"Less," said Jo. "They were a leading family back in the day, but not as prominent as the McKennas. The Hanrahans and the Reeses and the McKennas all married into one another's families, and traded servants back and forth and the like."

"Do you know anything about the servants who worked for the Hanrahans?" Martin piped up.

"Not really, I'm sorry to say," Jo answered. "They had plenty of live-in servants at one point, during the mid to late 1800s and early 1900s. That was very common for wealthy families then. But servants weren't really considered worthy of town gossip and there wasn't much in the historical society records from that time. More coffee, darling?" Jo refilled Sheriff Weaver's cup, and I buttered another biscuit.

Martin finally put his pen down long enough to eat a forkful of eggs. After he finished with his bite, he said, "Thank you so much for speaking with me." His eyes rested on me for a moment. "With us," he amended.

I felt my cheeks grow hot at the word "us."

Jo's eyes rested on Martin and me in turn and took on a mischievous gleam. "You two sure do make for a handsome couple," she remarked, turning her attention to her plate.

Martin abruptly made a noise somewhere between a cough and a strangled cry while I felt a flush creep up from my neck to my hairline. As a redhead, I blushed very easily and obviously.

"Oh, uh, we aren't really ... I mean, we're just, uh," Martin stammered.

"How are the wedding plans coming along?" I asked, frantic to change the subject.

"Things are wonderful," Sheriff Weaver said, sipping his coffee with a grin.

Jo chuckled. "Sure, all you have to do is put on your suit and show up. And you're wearing your dress uniform, so you don't even have to go shopping, you handsome devil." She turned to me. "Lacey, wait until you see my dress! It's an antique wedding gown, circa 1912, silk with a lace overlay and high collar. I'm going to wear my grandmother's cameo pin."

"Sounds gorgeous, where did you find something like that?" I responded.

"Etsy," she said breezily. "I found an antique gown dealer who does all her own alterations. I'm doing a quilt for her, and she's customizing the dress for me."

Jo made a very comfortable living designing and hand sewing spectacular custom quilts and selling them in her own Etsy shop. One of my proudest possessions was the wildly colorful patchwork quilt that Jo had given me when I graduated from college. I had broken it out from storage and put it on my bed after Jed moved out. He had called the quilt "vulgar" and "homemade looking" and, feeling embarrassed, I had promptly put it away in a storage trunk. I felt a sudden rush of shame, recalling how easily I had taken an item I loved, that meant something to me, and shoved it out of sight because my husband thought it looked ugly. *Was I really so willing to compromise myself like that?*

"Speaking of quilts," Jo interrupted my inner thoughts, "I have a bride's quilt that needs to get mailed out today, another Valentine's Day bride, and I simply have no time to run up to the post office. Would you two mind running it down there for me?" She looked from Martin to me expectantly.

"Of course, whatever you need," Martin said.

Jo rose from the table. "Bob, would you help me pack it up?" She and the sheriff left the kitchen together. I glanced up at the sunflower shaped clock on the kitchen wall.

"I have about an hour before I have to be at the library. I can drive it over to the post office, if you have other things to do," I offered. Martin looked offended.

"I'm coming along with you, of course," he said. I was feeling pleased that he was so adamant to accompany me, until he added, "I wouldn't miss a chance to check out the historic post office."

*   *   *

The Pinewood Corners post office was located in one of the oldest historic buildings in the heart of downtown. The structure dated back to the founding of the town, and was the site of the original mercantile and post that Merrick McKenna had built and operated back in the mid-1800s. While the current post office boasted all the updated amenities, the original heavy oak counter was still in place, lovingly maintained by the postmaster, Larry MacIntyre. I hadn't actually been in the building for quite some time.

The bell over the heavy wooden door with the leaded glass window jingled merrily as we pushed our way into the cavernous, yet cozy room. An old wood stove burned in the corner, creating a golden glow that reflected on the mellow gleam of the wooden paneling covering the walls. Martin looked around, his gaze trying to rest everywhere all at once as he took in the space.

Larry looked up from polishing the counter, the firelight reflecting off his bare scalp. He smiled, his large and bushy mustache contrasting with his bald head.

"Morning, folks. How can I help you today?" His tone was pleasant and welcoming. Larry liked to read science fiction and westerns, and his wife enjoyed checking out the home decor books. I returned his smile and briefly introduced Martin.

"We're here to drop off this quilt to be mailed," I said. "Mrs. Morten sent us."

"Of course, of course," Larry beckoned us over. "She called a few minutes ago, the payment is all taken care of."

Martin heaved the heavy wrapped box up onto the counter and dropped it on the surface. I could see Larry flinch at the impact on his beloved counter top. Larry did some typing on his computer and printed a label with a barcode that he affixed to the box. As Larry worked, Martin wandered away and was examining various details in the room.

I glanced over and saw him studying a shadow box mounted to the wall, an oversized frame that contained a display of various postcards, commemorative stamps, and letters from the founding days of the town on up to the present day. Several of the displays lined up along the wall that created a sort of timeline of the town. I hadn't paid attention to them in years, even though I was aware that Larry liked to occasionally change or update the materials in them.

"Hey, Lacey, this one has your name on it!" Martin's voice echoed across the room.

"What?" I turned my head and raised one eyebrow. I wasn't aware of anything with my name on it.

"Larry, where do you typically obtain these materials?" Martin asked without taking his eyes off the display he was studying.

"Oh, here and there," Larry replied breezily as he handed me the shipping receipt with the tracking number. "Sometimes people donate old items that they come across, sometimes I find random things tucked away that were misplaced decades ago." His impressive mustache raised at the corners. "Once, I even found a letter from the town's mayor to his cousin in Maryland dated 1914 between the floorboards and the counter when I was doing an annual cleaning."

"I guess the cousin never received *that* letter," I remarked with a laugh.

"Where did this one come from?" Martin asked, pointing to the glass he was standing in front of. I crossed the room to where Martin was standing, tucking the shipping receipt into my purse. I stopped and gazed at the item he was pointing to.

It was a postcard featuring a photo of a Mayan temple, with massive gray stone steps carved up the sides. The structure appeared as if it was being swallowed by the lush tropical greenery pressing in around it. The name "Lacey" was inscribed on the upper right corner of the photo in black marker, surrounded by a heart.

"What is this? Where did it come from?" I repeated Martin's question as I reached out and ran my fingers over the glass. My heart suddenly sounded very loud, pounding over the rush of blood whooshing through my ears. *That's my mother's handwriting.* I felt myself begin to sway on my feet as the light in the room shrank to a pinpoint.

Martin's hand grasped my elbow, and the warmth and strength of his grip pulled me back from the brink of consciousness. The room was bright with firelight again, and the rush of blood receded from my ears. I drew a deep, steadying breath and released it slowly.

Larry came out from behind the counter and joined Martin and me in front of the gallery wall. He produced a ring of keys from his front pocket. Selecting the smallest key, Larry unlocked the front of the wall-mounted case and reached in to delicately pluck the card from the backing. He flipped it over and examined it briefly before handing it to me. I took it with trembling hands and read the words written in my mother's familiar spidery, slanting cursive.

Darling Lacey,

I hope that you are doing well and being a good girl for your Aunt Denise. Your dad and I are both good, but we miss our little girl terribly. If all goes well, we will be home in time to celebrate your birthday next month—fingers crossed. I've got some wonderful surprises for you! This trip is proving to be very fruitful. Your dad and I are on the verge of something big, and I can't wait to tell you all about it. Now if we can just get the locals to get on board … Got to go now, my dear, we both love and miss you so much!

Love, Mom and Dad

I read and re-read the words several times. I was vaguely aware of a cold wetness on my cheeks and realized that I was crying when the letters began to blur. The postmark on the card was consistent with the time that my parents disappeared, and I realized that this was most likely the last postcard that they had ever sent to me.

"Larry, why didn't you tell me that you found this?" I clutched the card to my chest like a lifeline.

Larry looked at the tears rolling down my face and his brows drew together in distress. "I dunno. I guess I came across it and thought it looked like a cool picture and put it up on the display." His big brown eyes looked more hound-like than ever. "I'm sorry, I didn't really look at the back very closely. The name didn't seem familiar. Most of the time, the stuff I find is so old that nobody remembers the writer or the recipient, or the information is so out of date that it's just a quaint piece of history. You wouldn't believe the amount of stuff that falls through the cracks, literally." He looked genuinely upset, and I knew that I was being irrational.

The postcard didn't reveal the answer to what happened to my parents, nor did it contain information that would have averted their disappearance. Its simple message was just precious to me because I had so little left of them. Larry had transferred to Pinewood Corners five years ago to serve as postmaster and would have no idea of my history with my parents.

I glanced at the address and realized that it was addressed to my aunt's maiden name, and the house number was an apartment that she hadn't lived in for many years.

Larry awkwardly reached out and patted my shoulder. "Why don't you keep that, then? Seems like it's rightfully yours, anyways. Most of the things I find are addressed to places and people that don't even exist any more, so I just …" he trailed off.

"Thank you," I whispered, still hugging the postcard to my aching heart.

Larry closed and locked the display. "I'll be sure that package goes out today, Lacey. Let Jo know, would you?"

"Of course," I replied, blotting my face with my coat sleeve. The bell over the door chimed again as another customer arrived. Embarrassed at my emotional reaction to the postcard, I brushed quickly past the woman entering the building. The icy air was bracing and I breathed in huge gulps of it to clear my head. Behind me, the door chimed again and I turned my head and watched Martin exit the post office. He stepped up beside me and his brown eyes fixed on my watery green ones. I saw only support there, with no morbid curiosity.

"Do you want to talk about it?" he asked.

I turned away from him and the car beeped briefly as I reached into my coat pocket and hit the unlock button. "I need to get to work. Do you need me to drop you off somewhere?"

"I'll just walk over to the sheriff's station," he replied, pointing across the street.

"Oh, right," I half laughed at myself. Uncomfortable with the level of sympathy and about to cry again, I was suddenly desperate to escape Martin's gaze. I walked around my car and opened the driver's side door. I raised my eyes and he was still staring at me.

"I'll text you when I'm on my way later." The words came out in a tumble as I threw myself into the driver's seat and pulled the door shut with more force than necessary. I carefully tucked the postcard into my purse before I started the car. The last I saw of Martin was his slim form growing smaller as he walked in the opposite direction in my rearview mirror.

Chapter Ten

"**H**oney, why don't you go on, and I'll lock up for you. It's dead as a doornail in here, anyhow." Miriam's warm blue eyes behind her wire-framed glasses were sympathetic.

"Is it that obvious?" I asked her. We were both leaning on the checkout counter, chins in our hands, watching the clock count down the final hour until closing time. We hadn't seen a single patron in hours. Today was the opening day of the Sweetheart Soiree festival, and most folks were out having fun with the activities rather than stopping by the library.

"It's obvious that you've got something on your mind," Miriam said. "Want to talk about it?"

That was the second time today that someone had asked me if I wanted to talk about it. I looked at Miriam and sighed. *Maybe I should stop fighting the signs and accept a willing ear and a little support.*

"Can you keep a secret?" I asked.

She responded by drawing her brows together and making a *pffft* sound with her lips. "Girl, you know you don't even have to *ask* me that. Of course I can!" She crossed her arms over the bib of her worn denim overalls and gave off a highly offended air.

I tried for a reassuring smile in an effort to calm her down a bit. Leaning towards her, I said softly, "Martin and I stopped by the post office today, and Larry had this in one of those framed cases along the wall." I slipped the postcard from the pocket of my blazer and placed it carefully on the counter. Miriam leaned over and examined it, turning it over several times. She let out a long, low whistle.

"Wow, how did he come across this?" she asked.

"He said there's a lot of things that get stuck or lost that he finds around. He didn't remember exactly where this came from."

Miriam shook her head, sending her braids swinging. "It's wild how much human detritus there is to sift through in this world," she remarked poetically. "Does this give you any more clues as to whatever might have happened to your parents?"

"Not really, but it does give me some comfort to know that they were thinking of me and missing me in their last days," I replied, my voice catching.

"Of course they were, honey. I'm sure they loved you very much." Miriam gently patted my shoulder. Her compassion had a heartening effect and tears suddenly filled my eyes. I automatically pulled my emotions behind the invisible walls I had constructed around my heart many years ago as a survival mechanism. I stepped out of Miriam's reach and snatched up the postcard to replace it in my pocket.

"Anyway," I said briskly, "no point in wallowing in the past. Have you finished all the reshelving?"

Miriam looked cooly at me and leaned against the wall behind the counter. "Yes, I finished up a couple of hours ago. There weren't many reshelves, it's been quiet all day." By unspoken mutual agreement, we dropped the subject of my parents.

Changing the tone, Miriam said, "We've got some really good entries for the love poetry contest. Some are silly and fun, some are very romantic, and some are just plain goofy."

"I'm not looking at them," I said. "I want to be completely surprised and unbiased when I announce the winner and read the poem that the people voted for."

"There's still over a week left for the entries to come in." Miriam waited for my response but got none, so she changed the subject again. "How's your Aunt Denise doing these days?"

I smiled in spite of myself. I had been very lucky that my aunt had been willing to take me in and raise me after my parents were gone, even though she was only 22 years old at the time. My Aunt Denise was a vibrant woman full of life, and she had dedicated her youth to bringing me up. She had finally found a partner and her ideal career path after I had graduated high school.

"She's doing great, last I heard. Her life coaching practice and yoga and wellness studio in Blakely is doing a brisk business," I replied. "The space is just gorgeous. She brought back some amazing decor items from her honeymoon in India last year. Her new husband, Derrick, helped with all the set up and design of the studio. He teaches classes there as well."

"Your aunt and your parents both seem to have had quite the wanderlust," Miriam observed. "I wonder how it missed you?"

Her comment was innocent, but it gave me pause. I really didn't go anywhere, and I had made Pinewood Corners my sanctuary. But I was starting to wonder if it was my refuge or my confinement. I thought of Maeve McKenna, in her gilded prison of wealth and status, stalked by a man that threatened her and her family's very existence, and forced to leave behind her life of privilege and status. *Where had she gone? What had happened to her? How did she find the courage within herself to escape from her situation?*

Lost in my thoughts, I was startled when Miriam abruptly announced, "Here comes a patron!" She sounded as excited as she might have been if a celebrity had just walked through the doors.

I glanced up as the main doors opened and a familiar stocky blonde entered. She smiled sunnily at Miriam and I as she unwound her blue woolen scarf.

"Hi, Lacey, hi, Ms. O'Connell. It sure is cold out there, *whew*. I mean, it's February so of course it's cold, but there's a little bit of a wind going today so it adds to the cold. Makes it a little bit sharper, if you know what I mean. But that sure hasn't stopped anyone from going to the festival, no siree, main street is packed, and Chuck Smalls has opened the bowling alley early, it's all decorated for the festival, even the bowling pins have hearts on them, and you get twenty percent off a game if you have a red bowling ball, and the street vendors are serving hot chocolate and and mulled cider and mochas and funnel cakes with whipped cream and heart-shaped sprinkles, heart-shaped soft pretzels, and pink corn dogs—*pink* cornmeal batter, I never in all my life saw that, and just all kinds of fun things. There's dancing in the town square, of course, that's always popular, and they have those outdoor heaters all over the place, it's so festive, don't you think so?" Colleen finally had to stop for a breath. Her speech was always a stream of consciousness, and I wondered if she slept like a baby at night because she never had an unexpressed thought to cause her any stress or strain.

"Hi, Colleen. Nice to see you. Can we help you find anything?" I returned her smile, grateful for the distraction from my uncomfortable thoughts.

Colleen cheerfully hoisted a bulky canvas bag she was carrying. "I ran out of reading materials," she explained. She strolled over and plunked the bag on the checkout counter and began removing stacks of books. Miriam stepped up and scanned the books into the system as Colleen placed them on the desk.

"I'll just go and get these re-shelved," she remarked as she stepped away with her arms filled with books. "They're all from the same section." Her eyes sparkled with mischief as she wriggled her eyebrows up and down.

Colleen gazed at me with hope in her pale blue eyes. "Do you have any new romance novels?" she asked. "The spicier, the better! I mean, I think that's as close as I'll ever come to having a hot romance, is by living vicariously through my favorite romance novels." She uttered a self-deprecating chuckle.

"Don't sell yourself short, Colleen. Although in the meantime, I think I might have a few books that fit that criteria nicely." I beamed at her.

Before long, Miriam and I were waving at Colleen as she exited the library, her tote bag once again brimming with juicy romance novels. Colleen had announced her intention of stopping by a street vendor for a hot mulled cider and a heart-shaped soft pretzel to go so that she could go home and curl up in her favorite sweats with one of her newly checked out books, since she was off work from the Pet Palace for the next two days.

"That girl is a category-three hurricane of words," Miriam remarked as we watched Colleen climb into her nondescript sedan.

"Oh, be nice," I said, smiling to soften my words.

"I am being nice," Miriam said defensively. "She's actually a category five! Sweet girl, though, she's got a good heart."

"On that note, let's go ahead and close up a little early," I said.

Miriam sketched a mock salute. "Sure thing, boss!" She went to grab our coats and purses as I shut down the computers. As we were exiting the building, I paused while locking up. "Thanks, Miriam, for always being such a good volunteer—and friend." My eyes remained on the alarm key-pad as I spoke.

"You bet, honey," Miriam replied with a firm pat to my shoulder. "I'm going to check out some of the festivities this evening. See you around?"

"Yes, I'm going to pick up Claire, run home and change, and pick Martin up at the station, and we'll check out the festivities as well."

Miriam winked as she fastened the huge buttons down the front of her overcoat. The big beige coat didn't really match the rest of her hippie granny ensemble, but it somehow worked for her.

"That's fabulous. Maybe we'll run into each other." She turned to head to her truck and paused, looking over her shoulder. "You and that Martin fellow sure do make a handsome couple, if you don't mind my saying so." Her form disappeared in the fading evening light before I could reply.

*　　*　　*

"Mommy, why can't I wear my Princess Anna dress to the festival?" Claire asked me again. She was seated on my bed, with piles of discarded clothes around her, while I went through my closet trying to find something to wear.

"Because," I repeated patiently, "your Princess Anna dress isn't warm enough."

"But I can wear my winter coat over the top," she begged. Her tone was dangerously close to whining at this point.

"Claire," I said, trying hard to hold onto my temper, "you may *not* wear that dress tonight. You have a choice between your purple corduroys or your jeans with the unicorns on the pockets."

"Okay, Mommy! I want to wear my jeans!" Her mood suddenly swung to joyful acceptance as she bounded off the bed towards her own room. "I'm gonna wear my sparkly pink boots, too!" her voice drifted back down the hall.

Hmm … pink boots. I rummaged in the back of my closet on the top shelf and pulled out a pair of hot pink fluffy faux fur boots that came up to my mid calf. Jed had said that the boots looked like I had skinned the Pink Panther, hence the fact that they were tossed on the back of the top shelf of my closet. I decided to throw caution to the wind and plan my outfit around the boots. *In for a penny, in for a pound—and it's the opening day of the festival, so what the heck?*

Ten minutes later, I emerged from my room wearing a thick white turtleneck sweater with a thermal top underneath, a pale pink puffy vest, fleece lined pink leggings, a red knit hat and scarf, and the pink boots. I had slicked on some shiny red lip gloss, dusted an iridescent pink highlighter over my cheekbones, and slipped on my large, silver, heart-shaped hoop earrings.

"Mommy, you're so pretty!" Claire's voice was filled with awe. Well, I would be a hit with the under-five age group of girls, anyway. I observed that she had managed to get her jeans on, but she had paired them with a pajama top. Once she was changed and ready to go, we headed for the car.

"Are we picking up Mr. Martin?" Claire asked from the back seat.

"Yes, we are," I replied, shooting off a quick text to let Martin know we were on our way before I started backing out of the driveway.

"Yes!" I glanced in the rearview mirror in time to see Claire do a triumphant fist pump that made me laugh.

"Where did you learn to do a fist pump like that?"

"Miss Elaine does that when she's happy. She showed me how."

"Oh, did she? That was nice of her," I said. *Jed must be spending a lot of time with Elaine lately. Good for him.* The platitude gave me no comfort as I drove towards the downtown municipal complex, so I focused on the traffic and the pedestrians and all the detours set up to keep the cars off of main street, where the festival was taking place.

Once again, I pulled up to the curb as Martin stood waiting for me in faded nylon hiking pants with zippered pockets on the sides and his puffy olive green coat. He slid into the passenger seat in a rush of cold air and scents of sandalwood, leather, and vetiver. The man definitely smelled great.

"I thought you left a half hour ago?" he complained. *Smells great, sounds grumpy.*

"It took twice as long to get over here through the detours and the traffic," I said as I started to pull away from the curb.

"Wait," Martin put his hand on my knee. It felt like all the blood in my body froze for a moment at his touch. Then he noticed my outfit. "Whoa, you're a walking valentine," he said, laughter bubbling in his voice.

I held my head high and replied in a very dignified tone, "Yes, I am. Thank you for noticing." Seemingly on cue, the Valentine's playlist I had going switched to the classic Sam Cooke track, "Cupid." Neither Martin nor I could hold back our laughter any longer.

"What's so funny, Mommy? I like this song!" Claire piped up.

I wiped tears from my eyes and tried to catch my breath as Martin turned his attention to the back seat.

"Your mom is a very humorous lady," he told Claire.

"What's hoom-rus mean?" she asked.

Martin shifted his gaze to me and his brown eyes softened in a way that made my heart beat faster, and my blood went from frozen to rushing madly. "It means that she's a very funny and fun lady, and she makes me smile."

Somehow, the thought that I could make this studious, serious man smile made me feel powerful and proud.

"Why don't we leave the car here," Martin suggested, "in the municipal lot? My dad said that was okay. Then we can just walk around the festival."

I agreed with Martin's idea, since parking was always an issue with festivals. We left my car in the municipal lot and trooped back over to Main Street together. The streets were lit up with strings of pink and white fairy lights, portable heaters, fire pits, and heart-shaped lanterns everywhere. As Colleen had said, there were food and beverage vendors on every corner serving up all manner of love-themed treats. Dinner consisted of heart-shaped personal pan pizzas for each of us.

Claire was currently enjoying getting very sticky with a giant rice cereal treat nearly the size of her head, studded with heart-shaped cinnamon candies and red and white sprinkles. I had my gloved hands wrapped around a cup of hot cocoa, enjoying the warmth.

Martin had tried to find something "healthy" and ended up with a small bag of chocolate covered strawberries drizzled with a white candy coating. I suppose that was a healthier snack than the deep fried candy bars that were also sold at that particular booth.

Martin also carried a stuffed unicorn under his arm. He had won the prize for Claire by tossing a softball at oversized milk jugs. I had tried my hand at a darts game, with abysmal but hilarious results. We strolled along the sidewalks and took in the sights and sounds, the air redolent with the scents of frying oil and dough and sugar. Snippets of conversation, laughter and music were all around us.

Claire decided that she was done with the cereal treat, and I tossed the remains into a trash can and pulled a packet of wet wipes from my purse to clean her up.

"Hey, Lacey! And Martin, right?" I looked up from my task to see Jed holding hands with a woman with a short and glossy cap of dark hair under her festive fuzzy red ear muffs.

"Hi, there," Martin replied, reaching out to shake Jed's hand. He nodded a greeting to the woman, and Jed introduced her.

"This is my girlfriend, Elaine," he gestured proudly to the woman next to him and she smiled shyly at me and Martin and gave us a little wave.

"Hi Miss Elaine! I like your headphones!" Claire threw herself at Elaine, hugging her around the thighs.

"Thank you, they're actually ear muffs to keep my ears warm," Elaine said, affectionately patting Claire's head.

"It's a great festival this year," Jed remarked, his brown eyes sparkling over his pink cheeks as he squeezed Elaine's shoulders. Jed was smiling from ear to ear, and I thought that he was probably enjoying the Sweetheart Soiree more this year because of Elaine.

He looks really and truly happy. And to my surprise, I actually felt truly happy *for* him. Something in my heart broke free and I let it go, not even realizing that a major milestone had been reached and passed without fanfare. I was honestly thrilled to observe Jed's contentment with his new girlfriend and there was not a single pang of jealousy or regret. Things felt more right between my ex-husband and me than they ever had before, even when we had been married.

"Hey, princess, is that your unicorn?" Jed asked.

Without missing a beat, Martin dryly quipped, "Actually, I won it for Claire." Everyone burst out laughing.

"Well, I really like it," Jed said. "Hey, we were just heading over to the face painting booth, Claire. Do you want to come with us?"

"Can I, Mommy? Please?" Claire danced in place with excitement.

"Sure, if you want to," I told her. I glanced at Jed. "Where should we meet up afterwards?"

"If it's okay with you, I thought maybe we'd get our faces painted, have a caricature portrait done, maybe bowl a game and head home. Claire can hang out with us tonight and I'll drive her to school in the morning," said Jed.

"It's fine with me, if Claire's okay with the plan," I replied.

Claire's response was to throw herself at my legs and thank me profusely. Laughing, I untangled myself from a mass of excited little girl and gave her a hug.

Martin knelt down to hand her stuffed unicorn over, and to my surprise, she threw her little arms around him and gave him a fierce hug.

"Thank you for my Herbie!" she said.

"Uh, you're welcome," Martin replied with some understandable confusion.

"I think Herbie is the unicorn's name," I whispered loudly. Claire grabbed said unicorn and clutched it tightly.

"Let's go, Daddy!" she said, grabbing Jed's hand with her free one and tugging him away. "I wanna get a unicorn painted on my face. Can I get one?" Her bright chatter faded as they walked away.

"Well, I guess we're on our own," Martin stated the obvious. "What else did you want to do?"

"Let's just walk to the end of Main Street and see what else is going on, and we can stop by Mikki's bakery on our way out."

We passed more booths selling flashing heart necklaces and red, pink, and white glow sticks and the like, and even more food and treats. The kissing booth had a line halfway around the block. I had heard that Rayna had volunteered, along with the current Miss Pinewood Festival Princess and two very handsome eligible bachelors. The money earned went towards the Wingate County Community Food Pantry, so it was for a good cause.

"Wanna wait in line for a kiss from Rayna?" I teased Martin, elbowing him in his side.

"Nope, I'll pass," he replied placidly. "The line's too long."

I feigned outrage at his comment and pretended to stalk away. I only went a few steps, however, and Martin pulled me back, laughing.

"Hey, you two!" The shout had me glancing over to see Jo. We were near the town square, and Jo was dancing past us in the arms of Sheriff Weaver. "Come join us!" she called as they whirled by to "Accidentally in Love" by Counting Crows.

"Shall we?" Martin was holding his elbow out in an invitation. I hesitated, worried what I would look like and what people might think of the head librarian cutting it up on the dance floor. *Stop hiding and have a little fun for once!*

I threw caution to the wind and looped my arm through Martin's. Looking absurdly pleased, he led me onto the dance floor and the song changed to the upbeat and fun "I Gotta Feeling" by the Black Eyed Peas.

A rush of people flooded onto the dance floor, and we were swept to the middle. I started stomping my feet, clapping my hands, and shaking my hips to the rhythm of the music. Martin was also swinging his hips and gyrating his shoulders.

"Nice moves!" I shouted.

Martin grinned and did a little twirl in response. I was sweating in my winter gear by the time the song ended. As the tempo switched to a slow beat, a number of people drifted away from the dance floor as a handful of couples shifted closer together. I started to walk away when I felt Martin's hand on my elbow.

"Leaving so soon?" he asked.

"Well, I—" was all I got out before he pulled me closer to him and placed one hand on my shoulder as he kept ahold of my other hand with his and began to lead me in a slow sway around the dance floor. I felt numb from the waist down and told myself it was nothing more than the cold. I prayed that he couldn't hear my pounding heart over the steady beat of the music.

I realized that we were dancing to the classic 80s hit by Foreigner, "I Wanna Know What Love Is." As I swayed in Martin's arms, the significance of the lyrics hit me hard. I had been married and divorced, and I still questioned if I ever really knew what love was and if I had ever truly experienced it. Martin's breath brushed my temple and I shuddered.

"Are you cold?" He pulled me slightly closer to the warmth of his body. I wanted the song to be over, and yet I never wanted it to end. I didn't feel the cold at all, nor did I feel the floor under my feet as I floated in Martin's arms.

"I thought you didn't like music," I croaked out. My mouth was as dry as the Sahara Desert.

"I never said I couldn't dance," Martin breathed into my ear. I felt goosebumps erupt down the entire left side of my body. Before I could pass out, the song ended, and a more upbeat "You Make My Dreams" by Hall and Oates started to play. Martin stepped back and raised his eyebrows at me as if to ask if I wanted to keep dancing. I shook my head, too overwhelmed to speak yet.

He followed me as I wove my way between the dancers and left the floor. Out in the open, the air felt cold and crisp and wonderfully refreshing on my flushed cheeks. My knees felt like jelly, and I wasn't sure if it was from the dancing or from being so close to Martin. *It's from the dancing, all that exercise, nothing more, that's just silly. I barely know this man, for heaven's sake.*

"I'm thirsty," I told Martin. "Let's get some cider."

A few minutes later, we sat on a bench sipping hot cider and watching the crowds flow past.

"Is there more you want to do here, or are you ready to go?" Martin asked.

"Let's stop by the new MB Squared bakery," I responded.

Martin stood and offered his hand to help me up. "Let us adjourn to the bakery, Your Ladyship."

I laughed and waved his hand away as I stood and we made our way through the crowds to my friend Mikki's new bakery.

We waited in the line that snaked past the front of the building for almost half an hour. When we finally made it through the front doors, I spotted Mikki behind the counter. She had a heavy dusting of flour across the bib of her green apron, and over her right cheek. Her light brown hair was piled atop her head in a messy bun and she looked completely exhausted and thrilled. When she spotted me, she let out a joyful shriek and ran around the counter, leaving Michael temporarily on his own to serve and ring up the mouthwatering treats in the cases.

"Lacey, you made it!" Mikki threw her arms around me and gave me a brief squeeze. She smelled delicious, like chocolate, sugar, and butter.

"Wow, business looks brisk, congratulations," I said, squeezing her back. "I want some more of those petit fours."

"Oh, we sold out of those hours ago," Mikki informed me. "But we've got plenty of cherry chocolate chip cookies, sugar cookies, cake pops, and cupcakes."

"Cherry chocolate chip?" Martin sounded intrigued.

Mikki turned to him and grinned. "Yes, they've been a big hit—my famous bittersweet chocolate chip cookie recipe, with chopped dried cherries added."

"Sounds great, I'll take two," Martin enthused.

"Make that half a dozen," I said, and Mikki rushed off to fill the order.

Once we had our little bakery box of cookies in hand, I asked Martin what he wanted to do next.

"Well, how about we go back to your place and we can discuss what I've found in my research today?" His light brown eyes sparkled with anticipation.

"Okay, that sounds good. I wouldn't want to deprive you of discussing your research for too long." I shifted the box of cookies from one hand to the other so that I could grab my keys. "Shall we, then?"

Martin stood and sketched a deep bow. "Lead the way, my gracious lady."

Chapter Eleven

As we pulled into my carport, I waved to the sheriff's cruiser parked across the street.

"Wow, they're really taking this seriously," I remarked, shutting off the engine and cutting off Michael Bublé in mid-croon.

Martin sighed with what sounded like intense relief at the sudden quiet. "Yes, Janine probably threw some money at them. She likes to do that," he replied.

"I suppose that's a habit that would be easy to develop when you're raised with billions," I said, my tongue firmly in cheek.

Once we were in the house, I took care of the dogs' needs and I changed into my favorite purple leggings and pink and purple oversized sweatshirt. I went to the kitchen to put on a pot of water for tea. I had debated putting my unruly flame colored locks up, but thought that I looked better with my hair down. *Why am I worried about impressing this guy? He doesn't pay attention, other than to take note of some of my more outlandish outfits. I* put several peppermint tea bags into the gold and pink elaborately painted tea pot, looping the strings around the delicate handle. I focused on my task and tried to shake off my current train of thought.

I heard and somehow *felt* Martin enter the kitchen. I turned my gaze to him as he leaned against the counter and his eyes traveled from my head to my feet and back again. His lips twitched as he fought against the grin that was trying to pop out.

"Pink and purple shirt, purple pants, and blue and yellow striped fluffy socks?" He finally lost the battle and started to laugh.

"Hey," I cried, "at least I wear colors, Mr. Neutrals." I grinned back at him and waved one of my feet in the air. "And these aren't just socks, these are *toe* socks." I wriggled my toes for emphasis and Martin shook his head and laughed harder.

"Nobody makes me laugh like you do, Lacey," he said, catching his breath. I busied myself pouring the hot water over the tea bags and carefully placing the lid on the pot and avoided looking at him.

"So, about that research today …" I began.

"Lacey, I'm curious. I know you mentioned growing up with your aunt. What happened to your parents?" Martin asked. I looked at him, finally meeting his eyes.

"Why do you want to know?" I asked.

"Because I don't want to inadvertently say the wrong thing. Because I have all these scenarios playing in my head, like, maybe you were removed from their home for some reason, maybe you ran away, maybe your parents ran off and joined a cult—"

"My, you have quite the imagination," I rudely interrupted him, upset at the flippant tone of his voice. I threw the cabinet open and snatched up two mugs. "Let me put your curiosity to rest. It was nothing that dramatic. They simply up and disappeared, vanished into thin air. They—they abandoned me."

My voice broke on the last word as I slapped the mugs down on the counter and brushed past Martin, heading for the living room and away from this conversation. I felt a hot flush of humiliation coloring my cheeks. I threw myself down on the couch and grabbed the remote and aimed it at the television.

Martin sat in the club chair. "Lacey, I had no idea you went through that, or that you've interpreted the situation the way you have. You—"

I hit the volume button and turned the TV up loud enough to drown Martin's voice out. He kept shouting my name and asking me to turn the volume down. In response, I selected YouTube Music and clicked on a Nikki Minaj video.

Martin countered this by getting up, crossing the room in three long strides, and turning the TV off with the power button along the bottom. I aimed the remote and clicked again, but the set didn't pick up the signal with Martin standing in the way.

"I thought you wanted to discuss your research," I said icily. "Since when am I a part of your research?"

"I'm sorry, Lacey. I really didn't know, and we've been working together on this, and I thought maybe I should try to better understand you. I didn't mean to push you like that, I didn't know how you felt." He held his hands up, palms out, in a gesture of surrender.

I heaved a deep, shuddering sigh. "I suppose I overreacted, how could you possibly know how sensitive I am about this? It's been so long, I really should be over this by now."

Martin crossed the room again, more slowly, and approached me warily. "Do you really think they abandoned you?"

I pulled my feet up, tucking my legs under me. I couldn't look up and meet Martin's eyes. "It felt like that. Like they just decided not to come back. They were archaeologists, like you. Rationally, as an adult, I know they didn't intentionally leave me, but that eight year old girl, she felt like maybe there was something that she had done to drive them away … That postcard you found, what it said, about them wanting to be home in time for my birthday, that was the first time I felt like maybe they *did* want to return from Mexico and back to me."

My walls were cracking, I could feel something inside me swelling and pushing against the walls, finding the weaknesses and expanding the fault lines, eroding the fortress of the defenses I had constructed around my heart so many years ago. I felt the couch dip as Martin lowered himself onto the cushion next to me.

"I'm sorry," he repeated. He laid his hand on my shoulder and rested it there. He said nothing more for a time, and he didn't need to. Those two words were enough. His presence was enough in that moment as I waited to see if my walls would hold. After some time had passed, I decided that although there was extensive damage, the walls would stay up, at least for now. With a shudder and a hitch of breath, I squared my shoulders and bucked myself up.

"Listen," Martin said softly, "I could make some inquiries while I'm down in Mexico, maybe pick up a trail on what happened to your folks."

"I—I don't know. I mean, thank you and everything, but I'm not sure it would help. If something truly tragic happened, the details may be more devastating than not knowing."

"Okay, I understand. If you change your mind, just say the word." Martin gave my shoulder a squeeze before letting go. "How about that tea now? I need something to settle my stomach after all the festival food. Not to mention something to calm my nerves after that emotional outburst."

I shot Martin a watery smile, and his eyes crinkled at the corners as he smiled at me, accepting my change of subject without pushing. "You're a good friend, Martin," I said.

His eyebrows lowered and a troubled look passed over his face for the briefest instant. Had I only imagined seeing it?

"Sure, no worries," he mumbled as he busied himself with rummaging through his messenger bag.

Shortly, we were seated at my dining room table, sipping peppermint tea and surrounded by copies of Martin's research documents.

"A lot of Mary Elizabeth's journal writings were rambling snippets of poetry. I think they're autobiographical, but the meanings are difficult to decipher," Martin said, reaching out to grab a folder. He extracted a packet of papers and slapped them with the back of his hand.

"Like this entry—she references 'my darling boys' but the Hanrahans only had one son at the time, and four girls. And she had a daughter, apparently named Colleen. So who is she referring to?"

"Colleen?" I asked. "Now that's interesting. Did you know that the McKenna family had a tradition of naming the first born girl of each generation Colleen? It went way back to the family's roots in Ireland."

"I didn't know that," Martin sounded fascinated and began flipping through his notebook to add this new tidbit of knowledge.

"Mary Elizabeth even wrote little poems to these boys she keeps mentioning, and the last line of every one of these poems is the same. 'Remember ME with love.'"

"What does that mean?" I asked, puzzled.

"Not a clue," Martin growled in frustration.

"Do you recall that in Maeve's journal, she says that she booked passage under the name Julia Flaherty?"

I looked up from the pages I was examining. "Vaguely," I replied and took another sip of tea.

"Well, I looked up the passenger manifest of all the ships departing around that time, and there was no Julia Flaherty on any of them. There was a Julia Flaherty booked for departure on the *Adelaide* departing for England, but no one with that name ever checked in on board."

I had put down the papers and the teacup and was listening with rapt attention. "I wonder why she didn't check in? Did she sneak on board?"

"But why would she? She had a paid ticket." Martin stood and began to pace around the table, running his hands through his auburn hair and standing it on end. "Interestingly, one of the passengers was named John Paul Ryan. He booked at the last minute." Martin's amber eyes met mine.

"The mysterious JP?" I asked, raising one of my eyebrows.

"How do you do that? Never mind, don't distract me. I don't know," Martin sounded flustered as he waved his hands around.

"Maybe," I theorized, "Maeve found out that JP figured out her fake name and was following her." I got up and started to pace as well, warming to my story. "Maybe she leaked it on purpose, hoping he would try to follow her, and then she ditched the ticket, hoping to buy herself some time when he was on that ship!" I clapped my hands for emphasis, and I felt sure that I was right.

"Okay, so say you're right. Then where did she go? If this JP was gone, why wouldn't she just keep on living her life as Maeve McKenna?"

"That's the six million dollar question," I replied, tapping my chin. "I think she knew that JP would never stop, that she might be able to throw him off for a while, but not forever."

We went around and around, formulating theories and examining the pages of notes and copies. One of the more intriguing passages from the journal of Mary Elizabeth was the verse:

> *The treasure I carry more precious than gold*
>
> *Riches of which he must never know*
>
> *This secret I must forever hold*
>
> *I sit and I wait for him to go*
>
> *A new life built from ashes of the old.*

We went back and forth over possible interpretations, and even whether the passage was just a poem or a true message of some kind. Finally, I looked at my phone and noticed the time.

"Look, it's getting late. We've made some good progress for now. Why don't we watch some TV? How about a few episodes of *Supernatural?*"

Martin looked affronted. "Television? Now? Are you serious? I can't think of a more wasteful way to spend time, especially when—"

"Prolonged tension leads to poor results," I interrupted. "I heard that someplace."

Martin's scowl morphed into a smirk. "Must've been a very wise man who said that. You're right, of course. We need a reprieve to clear our heads."

We sat side by side on the couch, watching the first few episodes of the 15-season show. Martin pretended to be disinterested in the paranormal adventures of the fictional monster hunting brothers, Sam and Dean Winchester, but I could tell he was getting into the urban legend aspect of the show, and he was watching the screen with rapt attention. After the second episode ended, Martin turned to me.

"The legends of the Wendigo in Native American culture are fascinating. Did you know that—"

I grinned at him. "Getting into a 'frivolous' TV show?" I teased.

His face colored slightly. "I can admit to being wrong, on very, very rare occasions," he replied.

"Well, I'm hungry for a snack. How about some popcorn?" Without waiting for a reply, I got up and headed for the kitchen. As I passed the dining room table, I turned to ask Martin if he wanted a soda or more tea, and my hip accidentally bumped the edge of the table, sending pages drifting to the floor. I bent to pick them up and sort them back into their piles. I stopped, confused for a moment as I stared at two sets of pages.

"Martin, which copies are these?" I asked. Martin rose and made his way over to the dining room. He looked over my shoulder.

"Those must be from Mary Elizabeth's journal," he said, pointing at one of the photocopied pages covered with handwriting. "See, it's the same handwriting we've been studying all evening."

My hands began to tremble. "Martin," my voice was shaking, too. "I think these pages," I held up the papers in my right hand and shook them, "are the pages you copied from Mary Elizabeth's journal." I held up the pages in my left hand. "But these pages are the ones I copied from Maeve Eireen's journal, I'm sure of it. Look, she writes about her 'dear husband Merrick' here. But, Martin, the handwriting—it's *exactly* the same."

Martin peered closer, then snatched both sets of pages out of my hands. His eyes jumped back and forth between the documents, then he held the pages on top of one another up against the light.

"By God, you're right," his voice was tightly controlled but vibrating with excitement. "If this is accurate, it looks very possible that Mary Elizabeth and Maeve Eireen were one and the same person. Mary Elizabeth was Maeve's disguise. She lived out her life hiding in plain sight as a servant, so that she could watch her sons grow up and be out from under the thumb of JP. It's brilliant, actually."

I began to jump up and down in my excitement. "It makes sense!" I cried. "*Remember ME with love.* ME. It means *both* Mary Elizabeth and Maeve Eireen!"

Martin abruptly pulled out one of the dining chairs and sat down heavily, running his hands over his face.

"Do you know what this means? We may have solved what happened to Maeve McKenna all those years ago."

"What about her daughter? Was she JP's or was she Merrick's?" My eyes went wide as I drew in a sharp breath and snapped my fingers. "Oh my goodness, the treasure she carried that was more valuable than gold, that had to have been the baby! We have to find out if the daughter had descendents.

If she was Merrick McKenna's child …" I trailed off, leaving the implications unsaid.

"If she did, there could be living McKenna descendents," Martin supplied the details I hadn't spoken.

"Well, I hate to rain on our little parade, but we still haven't found any details about the necklace."

Martin waved away my statement. "Now that we're operating on the hypothesis that Mary Elizabeth and Maeve McKenna were the same person, we can go over the verses in the journal with a fine-toothed comb. I think that those poems of Mary Elizabeth's were put there as clues, since she couldn't exactly come out and say things outright."

"That's true," I said, stifling a yawn. After the sudden adrenaline rush, I was crashing fast.

"You're tired, I should go." Martin's eyes were still shining with excitement.

"It's probably a good idea to sleep on it and maybe we'll have some new insights in the morning," I agreed. "Just let me grab some shoes and I'll drive you to the B&B." I yawned again.

"Are you okay to drive?" Martin frowned slightly with concern.

"Oh, yeah, I'm a mom. I can wake myself up in an instant when it's necessary," I assured him.

A few moments later I returned to the room wearing my bright green Crocs over my blue and yellow striped socks.

"Do you ever match your casual clothes?" Martin asked me.

I gathered up my purse and slipped into my coat. "Matching," I informed him, "is for losers." I winked and headed out the door as I heard Martin's pleasant laughter echoing from behind me.

Chapter Twelve

I woke up to a text from Martin. I snuggled into my bed, clutching my phone and grinning from ear to ear, feeling like a teenager again as I swiped open my texting app.

Morning, hope you had a good night's rest. Thanks for all your insights so far, I couldn't have come this far without you. I'll be going over the journals and documents today, I'll call you if I find anything significant.

Well, it wasn't exactly a romantic declaration. So why was I disappointed? I didn't need a romance, I needed to figure myself out first. The morning silence lay over the room like a heavy cloak. I glanced at the time and debated trying to go back to sleep. Finally, I swung my legs over the side of the bed and stretched my arms overhead. I slipped into my house slippers and my fuzzy robe and headed to the kitchen. The dogs followed, eager for their morning bathroom break and their kibble.

After taking care of the dogs, I brewed a strong cup of English breakfast tea and sipped it as I munched on a piece of cinnamon toast. The warm and earthy spice sweetened with sugar and combined with the salty melted butter was exactly what I needed to fortify me on a cold February morning.

I sighed with contentment as I sank back into the couch with my teacup. I eyed my journal, sitting on the side table. I still had some time before I had to get in the shower and get ready for work, so I reached out and set the teacup down and picked up my journal, running my fingers over the sumptuous velvety cover before opening the book and starting to write.

The old expression "be careful what you wish for" seems particularly poignant to me right now. I've been feeling lonely and out of sorts, and I did wish for a companion, a partner to share my life with, but now that I'm spending so much time with Martin, I have to wonder exactly what I was thinking of when I made that wish.

I do like Martin, he can be so funny when he's not trying to be so serious, he's intelligent, he listens without spewing useless platitudes about my parents, and he seems to respect my ideas and opinions. He even seems to be getting used to my eclectic sense of style.

But is it really a romance that I want? Or is it the support of a good friend? I'm scared of changing our budding relationship. It seems good right now, but so fragile at this stage. If I let Martin into my heart, will the romance kill the friendship? I would hate to lose him from my life because of a foolish desire to give into the weakness of being lonely and missing being in the arms of a man. Nothing ruins a friendship faster than a failed fling.

Anyway, Martin certainly hasn't made any clear moves in that direction. And if we are friends, I suppose my wish for a companion has been fulfilled—just not in the way I originally thought. I should be content with my life that is filled with good friends, a fulfilling career, a wonderful daughter ... if I try hard enough to be grateful for what I do have, maybe I won't lament that one small thing I don't have.

Martin is leaving for Mexico after Valentine's Day, anyway. I just can't deal with a broken heart. It would be better to stay single and focus on raising my little girl and running the library. Look at Maeve, she made such a sacrifice to save her sons and her unborn daughter and she lived her life out as a maid and a celibate single mom. She was strong, and I can be strong, too.

I closed the book with a sigh, content with my decision to stay the course as a strong and single woman as I headed to my bathroom to get ready for the day.

*   *   *

Later that morning, as I was reading *The Cat in the Hat* for the story hour in the brightly colored children's section of the library, Agnes rushed up and knelt down next to my chair.

"I'm sorry to interrupt," she leaned towards me and whispered loudly, "but there's a call for you at the main desk. It's that Martin fellow. He said he tried your cell but couldn't reach you, and he said it's *urgent.*" Her hazel eyes were wide.

I glanced at the children seated on the floor, waiting for the story to continue. I stood and thrust the book towards Agnes. "Thank you Agnes. Please take over, we left off on page seven."

Agnes took the book and settled into the chair I had vacated. As I hurried towards the desk, I heard her animated voice recounting the adventures of the infamous cat in the hat and I couldn't help but smile. Agnes was an excellent narrator.

As I reached the desk, I saw the red blinking light on the phone. I took a deep breath and squared my shoulders before picking up the handset. With a trembling finger, I punched the flashing button.

"This is Lacey," I said. I barely got the words out before Martin's breathless voice gushed over the line.

"Lacey, did you get my text? I think I'm on to something!"

"No, I was doing story hour with the children, and my phone is in my purse, in my office."

"Go get your phone, I texted you a picture of a verse. I'll hold."

I didn't bother hitting the hold button, I just dropped the handset onto the desk and ran for my office. I threw open the door and grabbed my purse. I pawed through and grasped my phone. The screen showed several missed calls from Martin, and a text. I swiped up. The text was a photo of a journal page. I tapped the picture to enlarge it and studied the words:

Six feet under soon here lies

Hiding under the place

Where a life is summarized

Behind the cracker barrels

And shovels on the walls

The treasure trove calls.

Here you will find me

Resting in my case

Reach me by entering

The most romantic of dates.

I read the verse several times, my mind racing. Forgetting all about Martin on hold at the desk, I opened the contacts on my cell and hit a number. My foot tapped impatiently as I waited for someone to pick up the line.

"Pinewood Corners Post Office, this is Larry speaking, how can I help you?"

"Larry! It's Lacey calling." My words came out in a rush.

"Hey, there, Lacey! What's up?"

"Larry, those shadow boxes, on the back wall—how long have they been there? Are they original to when the post office was operating as McKenna's mercantile?"

"Oh, I put most of 'em up after I took over as postmaster. I just thought they looked so cool, you know? A perfect place for displaying the history of our post office!" He sounded awfully proud.

My heart sank. "So none were there before this century?" I asked.

"There was one up when the building was being converted. That's where I got the idea. The mercantile had one up, to notify the community of births and deaths. That's where they would display the town's obituaries, mostly. I asked that it be left up, and I added the others. The walls are all the original wood paneling, you know."

"Larry, I'm coming down there now. I'll see you in fifteen minutes." I hung up before Larry could respond. I snatched up my purse and ran for the doors.

Agnes spotted me and called out, "What did he want?"

I remembered that Martin was still waiting on the line, and I yelled over my shoulder to Agnes, "He's still on the line. Tell him to meet me at the post office right away! And you're in charge, Agnes. Thanks!"

Less than fifteen minutes later, I roared up to the post office in my car and swerved to the curb. I jumped out, leaving the car parked crooked as I ran for the doors. A sheriff's cruiser pulled up and Martin popped out of the passenger door just as the vehicle rolled to a stop. To my surprise, Deputy Tom Willis climbed out from the driver's seat.

"What's this about some emergency at the post office?" Tom asked, placing his dark brown wide-brimmed hat on his head as he strode towards me.

"Tom, I think Martin and I have figured out something important," I said. I turned and went inside the post office, beckoning the two men to follow.

Larry looked up, startled at the sight of the three of us bursting through the doors. "Hey there, Lacey. What's going on?"

"Which one of the shadow boxes is the original one?" I asked, heading to the back wall.

"First one on the left. I had the frame changed to match the others, but it's the original," Larry said, pointing.

I approached the shadow box. "Can you unlock it, please?" I turned to Larry. He was already halfway across the room, keys in hand.

"Wait a second, Lacey. I think what we're looking for isn't inside, it's more likely to be behind it." Martin started knocking on the wall around the display.

"What in Sam hill is going on here?" Tom asked, hands on his hips. "Martin comes flying out of one of the evidence rooms like his hair's on fire, demanding a ride to the post office for some sort of emergency, and now you're trying to get behind the walls?"

"I hope we won't have to cut into the paneling, it looks original," Martin said.

Larry wrung his hands. "What's this about? I won't have my post office damaged!"

Tom stepped forward. "Why would you have to damage anything? What's going on?" he repeated.

Martin stopped his tapping and his gaze shifted from Tom to Larry. "I had a hunch, and when Lacey told me to meet her at the post office, I knew my hunch was correct. I know that in the small towns in the 19th century, general stores and the like were the community centers, along with the churches, and a lot of announcements would have been posted there. I also knew that Maeve's husband owned this building when she disappeared."

"That information does not make this situation any clearer to me," Tom said dryly.

"What he's trying to say," I explained, "is that we think Maeve's famous necklace might be hidden behind that wall." I pointed with a shaky finger.

Tom's jaw dropped. "Well, I'll be ..."

"We have to find a way to get this down," Martin patted the display.

"I think I can help with that," Larry said. Between the two men, they managed to unbolt the shadow box display from the wall. As they lifted it away, a square hole cut out of the paneling was revealed.

Martin peered in, shining the flashlight from his phone into the opening. "There's something here. It's some sort of lockbox!" He handed Larry his phone and carefully extracted a small metal box, rusted and filthy. A padlock dangled from the hasp that held the box closed.

"It's a combination lock," Martin reported. "I wonder if we can break the lock if we can't open it with the combination."

"Wait, try their wedding date—the day Maeve and Merrick were married," I said. I Googled furiously on my phone. "Try 06-18-60."

Martin fiddled with the tumblers, turning the stiffened numbers. He tugged and the lock held. Everyone in the room exhaled collectively and Larry offered, "How about Maeve's birthday?"

I looked up from my phone. "It's 10-12-42."

This combination also proved to be incorrect.

"Larry, do you have any tools? Maybe we can cut the lock or cut into the box—"

"Wait," I said. "I think I may have it. Try 02-14-65."

Martin's eyes lit up, the flecks of gold dancing as he grinned at me. "'Reach me by entering the most romantic of dates.' Of course! That's the date that Merrick was going to give her the necklace, Valentine's Day. You're brilliant, Lacey—I could kiss you!"

I felt my heart leap into my throat at the idea of him kissing me as Martin worked at the tumblers stiffened by the passage of a century and a half. I didn't realize that I was so tense until the hasp of the lock popped open and I exhaled in a rush. The silence of anticipation in the room was palpable as Martin pried open the lid to reveal a second metal case. This one was fancier than the utilitarian outer box. It looked like it was made of silver, but blackened with heavy tarnish.

Martin pulled a small penknife from his pocket and pried at the lid. After a considerable struggle, the lid gave way and popped open. Just as he reached in to pull out the contents, the bell over the door jingled merrily. Colleen Perkins shuffled into the building in a puff of cold air, her plump arms filled with boxes. She blew her curly blonde bangs out of her eyes.

"Hi there, Larry, I'm here to mail out these packages for the pet lovers club. I love that club, the members are so nice. Of course, I love an animal lover! Because I'm an animal lover, too. That's why I work at the Pet Palace, although I would love to own an inn that catered to pet owners, like a pet-friendly bed-and-breakfast, you know? We would have homemade treats for the pets and everything." She paused for breath and looked up, noticing the four of us standing there in front of a hole in the wall. Martin stood stock-still, and dangling from his hand was a sparkling heart-shaped ruby necklace surrounded by diamonds. I had never seen Colleen speechless before. Without uttering another word, her eyes rolled back in her head as the packages slid from her arms and she collapsed onto the floor.

*   *   *

"I'm fine, really," Colleen insisted as the EMTs examined her. "It was just such a shock! I looked up and there it was, Maeve McKenna's famous missing necklace. I mean, we've all heard the story so many times, everyone knows what that necklace was supposed to have looked like, I would know it anywhere, and you probably would have, too—anyone around here would know, for gosh sakes." The EMTs patiently loaded Colleen onto a stretcher and took her out to the ambulance. From her steady stream of chatter, I knew that she was going to be just fine.

I stood at the back of the room with Martin as Tom took possession of the necklace and case in an evidence bag. He had explained that the sheriff's department would take the jewelry into custody until the question of ownership was settled.

"I wonder who owns it? What will happen to it?" I mused. Martin simply shrugged.

"It really is all about the hunt for you, and the discovery, isn't it?" I nudged Martin playfully.

"Technically," Larry chimed in, "the law of 'treasure trove' holds that property that is considered precious and is hidden with no proof of its former ownership belongs to the finder, which is you." He tipped his head to indicate Martin.

"I couldn't have found it without Lacey's help," Martin said, "and we do know who the former owner was."

"But the McKennas have no living descendents," Larry said. "It's a shame." He shook his balding head.

"Oh, I might have some ideas about that," Martin said cryptically. He turned to me. "Can I speak with you outside for a minute?"

"Uh, sure, I guess." I followed Martin outside just as a familiar bright red Lexus pulled up to the curb. *Rayna. I should have known. She has a police scanner and would know something was up.*

"Talk fast, we're about to be ambushed by the so-called press," I muttered.

"Listen, I'd love to buy you dinner, to celebrate," Martin smiled tentatively at me.

"Tonight?" I asked, dumbfounded.

"If you're free, yes."

I tried to pinpoint my feelings, which were all jumbled between the excitement of finding the necklace and Martin inviting me to dinner. I felt exhilarated, apprehensive, and nauseous all at the same time. I took a deep breath and tried to calm and center myself.

"Okay, then. We'll have a nice, friendly celebration," I said. Martin's brows drew together and his mouth opened but before he could say anything, a recorder was shoved into the space between us.

"Well, well. From what I've heard, it looks like you get to keep your job after all. This is great publicity for Pinewood Corners. Now, tell me, on the record, how did you manage to solve the great puzzle of the missing necklace?" Rayna grinned like the Cheshire Cat and hit the record button and waved the machine impatiently.

Somehow, between the two of us, Martin and I cobbled together the story of how he had found the connection between the Hanrahan family and their maid, and how the identity of the maid had been uncovered and the connection made to the hiding place of the legendary necklace.

Rayna tried to steer the story towards a more sensational tone, and I had no doubts that the resulting article would be filled with the worst kind of purple prose. Martin would probably end up looking like Indiana Jones and Howard Carter combined. *He's going to hate that.*

"What are you smiling about?" Martin asked as Rayna climbed into her car to rush back to the paper to publish her scoop.

"Nothing," I waved him off. "Where did you want to have dinner? The El?"

"Oh, I think we can do better than that," he replied. "How about I pick you up at seven? I'll borrow my dad's car. His personal car, not the cruiser."

I laughed, picturing us screaming down the street with lights and sirens. Tom approached us.

"Good news," he said. "I just got word that your mysterious white car was found outside a motel in Greenwood. The driver and his accomplice were hiding out up there, waiting for things to blow over. They surrendered without a fight. They've admitted to being hired to follow you, but we don't know who hired them yet. The point is, you don't have to worry about them any longer."

"Unbelievable!" I cried. "That is great news! Could this day get any better?"

Martin smiled at me, his eyes crinkling at the corners. "Wait until dinner tonight."

Chapter Thirteen

"What about that dark blue dress? The one with the sparkles?" Mikki's voice was muffled as she was currently burrowing into the back of my closet.

"No, that dress is too fancy. I don't want to be over-dressed," I replied from where I was seated on the edge of my bed. "Don't you need to be down at the bakery with Michael?"

"I told Michael I had a best friend emergency. He under-stands. Everyone in town is talking about your incredible find today. Ha! I found it!" Mikki's voice rose in triumph.

"The blue dress?" I asked.

"Nope," Mikki emerged from the closet with a swath of black fabric draped over her forearms. "This one!" She held the fabric up and I recognized the black dress that I had worn to last year's Cupid's Ball. I had gone stag, with Miriam and Agnes. The dress was a black velvet with spaghetti straps and a subtle pattern of black hearts burned into the velvet. The hemline hit just above the knees.

"I'll freeze in that," I protested.

"You can wear tights and your black heeled boots and a wrap," Mikki insisted. "You look great in this dress." She pushed the bundle towards me. "You haven't had a date since … well, since Jed asked you to go together when we were fifteen. You should go all-out!"

"But that dress is kind of sexy, and this is not a date, he's just thanking me for my help with everything. I don't want to lead anyone on, Mikki. We're just friends. And just because you're deliriously happy and in love doesn't mean everyone else wants to be."

Ignoring my protests, Mikki steered me into the bathroom. "Now, we need a hairstyle that's cute but not too *cutesy*, if you know what I mean. Where are those tortoiseshell combs I gave you for your birthday last year?" Without waiting for an answer, she started rummaging through my bathroom drawers. "Sit down on the toilet lid, I'll do your makeup."

I wasn't going to win this argument. With a resigned sigh, I sank down onto the toilet seat lid. "The combs are in the top drawer," I muttered.

*   *   *

It was almost seven. I paced in my tiny entryway, then forced myself to sit down before I made myself all sweaty. I was wearing the black dress with thick black opaque tights and tall black boots with a skinny heel.

The dogs were agitated by my nervous energy. Jethro sat on the floor next to the couch and whined as he leaned against my leg. I patted him, hoping that I wasn't picking up his hair on my tights.

"Hey, off!" I shooed Elly May away from where she had curled up on my black and gold wrap. I shook the evidence of her presence off the wrap and draped it over my shoulders just as I heard a car pull up outside. I expected a text or a honk, so I was surprised when the doorbell rang. I tottered over to the door on my heeled boots and opened it tentatively, my heart hammering in my throat.

I peeked out to see Martin, looking breathtakingly handsome in black slacks and a gray sport coat that emphasized his broad shoulders and narrow waist. He wore a crisp, white dress shirt, open at the collar. And he was carrying a large bouquet of wildflowers. His wavy hair tumbled boyishly over his forehead, and his beard looked freshly trimmed.

"Wow, you look …" his eyes traveled up and down from my head to my toes. "You look … wow."

"Thanks," I pulled the wrap tighter around myself, feeling suddenly shy. "You clean up pretty well yourself. Are those for me?"

"Oh, yes, these are for you," looking startled, he held the apparently forgotten flowers out to me and I took them.

"Thanks, they're pretty. I'll just toss these into a vase and we can get going." I walked into the kitchen and Martin followed.

I pulled a vase down from one of the cabinets and began filling it with water from the sink. "You know, we're apparently the talk of the town after finding the necklace."

"I'll bet. That's why we're going somewhere a little more private this evening." His amber eyes glittered under the pendant lights. My heart skittered in my chest and I almost fumbled the vase. Somehow, I managed to get the flowers into the vase and the vase onto the dining room table.

Martin gallantly held my elbow as we walked down the slippery pathway to his father's long beige sedan. He led me to the passenger door, opened it, and held my arm to lower me into the car. It was an odd feeling to be handled so carefully, as if I were one of the delicate wildflowers, but I found that I sort of liked being treated as if I were something valuable and precious.

We drove in silence, and Martin glanced over at me, his face glowing orange in the dashboard lights. "Did you want some music?" He reached out and turned the radio on. To my surprise, he put on a pop station.

I smiled and tapped my knee in time with the music, and sang along with the chorus. I felt much more relaxed by the time Martin slowed the car down as we were pulling up to the B&B.

"Did you forget something in your room?" I asked.

In response, Martin shut off the car. "Stay put," he said as he exited. I watched him walk around the front of the car and over to my door. He opened the door and held his hand out to me, palm up, just as he had the first time we had dinner together. This time, I reached up and slipped my hand into his. An electric shock sparked through my palm, all the way up my arm, as he helped me out of the car. *Static electricity, that's all. Happens all the time in the winter.*

Martin guided me up the path and up onto the porch of the rustic building. He opened the double doors and a smiling woman greeted us with a sly, knowing smile. It was Andrea Wells, the proprietor of the PC B&B. She waved us off and told us to "have fun." I was mortified. What did she think was going on?

Martin led me up the stairs and down to the end of a hallway. I swallowed nervously as he opened the door, and we stepped into a room filled with candlelight. Elegance and charm filled the space. A small table set with a linen table-cloth and napkins, china, ornate silverware and crystal goblets caught my attention. *This must be the room he was staying in. Private, indeed.*

Martin took my wrap and hung it on the hook inside the door. He pulled out one of the chairs at the table, and I settled into it. The plates were covered with silver cloches, which Martin removed with a flourish.

"Voila," he announced. "Dinner is served." He sketched a bow. I looked down and saw what looked like chicken marsala with some sort of rice or risotto side and green beans.

I smiled with delight. "I love chicken marsala, it's one of my favorites. How did you know?"

"I may have stopped by the bakery for a quick chat with your friend Mikki."

I was incredibly touched that he had gone out of his way to find out what I liked to eat.

"I didn't make it, of course, Mrs. Wells made it," he clarified.

"It's still a lovely thought, and a lovely meal," I assured him. I picked up my knife and fork.

"Wait a second," Martin said, reaching for an ice bucket on the nearby sideboard. "We can't forget the celebratory champagne."

The bottle he pulled out made me gasp. *A bottle of Cristal? What was that worth? A thousand bucks?*

"That's an *expensive* champagne," I said with awe.

"Courtesy of Janine," Martin explained as he twisted the cage from the cork and worked it out with a satisfyingly loud pop. "She heard about our find and sent the bottle to the B&B."

"To you?"

"To us," Martin clarified as he poured the sparkling pale golden liquid into two crystal flutes. "To us," he repeated, holding his glass aloft.

I picked up my glass and clinked it to his. "To our find, and to Maeve," I said and we sipped. The champagne was smooth and tart and bubbly and delicious. I held my flute up to the candlelight and examined the bubbling liquid with interest. "Wow, I didn't even know that I liked champagne. This is way better than the ten-dollar stuff I occasionally get at the Fresh Stop."

Martin laughed and we dug into the meal, which was excellent. We talked easily about the events of the day, and the upcoming wedding of his father. I was invited as a guest, of course, as I had known Jo Morten since I was a little girl. Martin would be standing up for his dad, along with his older brother. Mikki would be the maid of honor. The ceremony would take place in the Grace Chapel just off Main Street, and the reception would follow immediately at the Cupid's Ball.

The conversation flowed, and gradually, the plates and the champagne glasses were empty and the candles had burned down. The atmosphere in the room turned suddenly from light and relaxed to moody and intense. Martin drained the last drops of his champagne, set the glass down, and leaned across the table.

"Lacey, I hope that this dinner begins to convey how grateful I am to you for your help, with everything. I could never have come this far without you and your insight, intelligence, and humor." He leaned even closer, until the golden flecks floating in his irises were clearly visible. I leaned back slightly.

"Sure, of course. I mean, I'm a librarian, it's what I do. Head librarian, in fact. That's my job, helping patrons with research. Also with finding books. That's one of the things I love about being a librarian, getting to help people, because people need help." *For goodness sakes, I sound like Colleen the way I'm rambling.* I plucked nervously at the linen napkin in my lap, my eyes cast downward.

"Lacey, look at me." Martin's voice was low and his tone was unmistakable. I slowly lifted my eyes to his. He got up and came around the table to me, his eyes never leaving mine. He knelt and took one of my hands in his and brushed his lips gently across the back of it. I tried not to shudder visibly as a jolt of energy shot through my entire body.

Martin kept a hold of my hand as he leaned towards me, his lips cruising up my arm towards my face. The flutter of his breath made my skin erupt into goosebumps. My heart was exploding and I could hear nothing but the rush of blood in my ears. *If I kiss him, everything changes, my relationship with Martin, the way I see myself, my entire life changes, it's the point of no return. No return, no return, no return, no return.* The words seemed to hammer into my brain with every heartbeat. My pulse throbbed in my throat as my head leaned back and a small moan escaped.

Martin's lips hovered over mine, and I could feel his breath and the bristle of his beard tickling my face. The scent of leather and woodsmoke and champagne engulfed me. His lips parted and as he leaned in, I jumped up so suddenly that my chair toppled over. I put my hand out and pressed it to his chest.

"I can't do this, I'm not ready. This isn't right. I—I'm sorry," I whispered, my voice constricted by the drumming of my heart in my throat. I fumbled around, grabbing my purse and snatching up my wrap without bothering to put it on. I ran from the room and flew down the stairs. I didn't look back as I flung open the front door and ran out into the frozen night.

*   *   *

"Thanks for picking me up," I said as the truck pulled to a stop in front of my little house.

"Sure, no problem," Mikki replied. "You saved my neck when I was overwhelmed and ran from the baking contest before. What are best friends for?"

"I can't even explain what happened."

"You don't need to. But if you want to talk about it, I'm here." She gave me a brief, hard hug. She smelled comforting, like cinnamon and vanilla.

"Thanks, Mikki," I whispered, giving her hand a final squeeze. The tears were going to start soon. I walked into my house, peeled out of my fancy clothes and left them in a wadded up pile on the floor, washed my face, put on my old comfy robe, indulged in a good long cry, and went to bed. I checked my phone right before I fell asleep. There were no messages.

*   *   *

The week went by, the time passing with no regard to my misery. I was surprised at how much I missed Martin's company and how quickly I had adapted to having him in my life. Claire asked about "Mr. Martin" every day, and I just told her that he was busy. I fended off several reporters trying to interview me about the "amazing discovery of a lifetime" of the necklace. I referred them to Mayor Reese, who was happy to take the spotlight.

I was closing up the library with Miriam the day before the Cupid's Ball and Jo and Sheriff Bob's wedding.

"No word from that Martin fella yet?" she asked me as I slipped my phone back in my pocket after checking it for the tenth time that hour.

"What? I was just, uh, checking the weather," I said defensively.

"Mmm-hmm," Miriam said, gesturing to the huge front windows. "Looks like it's clear and getting dark outside." She was wiping down the desk. "Why don't you call him? Or text, or Slack or TikTok or whatever it is you kids do to communicate these days?" she asked.

"I think I really screwed this one up, Miriam," I confessed. "I was so afraid to destroy our friendship with romance, and now I've just completely destroyed everything. It doesn't matter, anyway, he's leaving after the wedding tomorrow and I'll probably never see him again."

Miriam pursed her lips. "Oh, I don't know about that," she said slyly.

"What do you know? Have you heard something?"

Miriam suddenly pivoted subjects. "Have you been reviewing the entries for the poetry contest?"

Startled at the sudden change in conversation, I replied, "No, I want to be surprised as everyone else when I announce the winner that the other patrons have chosen. Agnes is keeping track of everything."

Miriam cryptically smiled and said nothing as we finished our closing duties. As we walked out to the parking lot together, she asked me what I planned to wear to the ball tomorrow night.

"Oh, jeez, I've been so scatterbrained this week that I haven't even thought about it," I said, smacking myself on the forehead. "I can't wear what I wore last year." *I'll never be able to wear that dress again, it will always remind me of that evening with Martin.*

"What about that sparkly blue number?" Miriam asked. "Agnes and I are both wearing matching pantsuits, except mine will be pink and hers will be red."

I grinned in spite of myself at the mental picture. I was so lucky to be able to work with those two ladies.

"I'm sure I'll figure out something," I said as we reached our vehicles. "Goodnight, Miriam."

Miriam climbed into her rusted pickup with a wave and drove off in a cloud of exhaust.

Chapter fourteen

The next day dawned bright, clear and cold. I stood in my closet after lunch, trying to decide what to wear to the wedding and the Cupid's Ball. I didn't want to go, truth be told. I really just wanted to stay in bed and watch old movies and eat cookies, but I couldn't miss Jo's wedding, and I had to be at the ball to announce the winner of the love poetry contest. Agnes would go into palpitations if I asked her to do it, and the thought of folksy, practical Miriam reading a love poem aloud made me shudder.

Claire appeared in the closet doorway.

"Mommy, *Frozen* is over. Can I watch *Moana* now?"

I smiled at my little girl, observing a rim of chocolate smeared all around her mouth.

"Did you eat the rest of the cherry chocolate chip cookies?" I asked her, my hands on my hips. She shook her head solemnly.

"No, Mommy," she said, her green eyes, so like my own, were wide with innocence.

"Really? Well, why don't we wash that chocolate off your face and pack a bag for you? Your daddy is coming to pick you up and drop you off at your Grandma Sue's house."

Claire jumped up and down and clapped her little hands. "Yay, Grandma Sue lets me stay up late and drink soda and eat caramel popcorn!" She dashed off towards the bathroom to wash up. I shook my head. Jed's mother was a pushover with her granddaughter, and I couldn't really blame her.

Jed picked Claire up about an hour later, and I was still in my fuzzy bathrobe, trying to decide what the heck I was going to wear. I was on the verge of just putting on the darned sparkly blue dress when a flash of red caught my eye.

I pawed through my closet full of clothes and yanked out a wire hanger poking out from a dry cleaners bag. Peeling the thin layer of plastic away from the slinky full-length dress, I remembered the only time I had ever worn it.

Before Claire was even born, I served as a bridesmaid in my college roommate's wedding. The illusion neckline over the sweetheart bodice flattered my figure perfectly. Sliding my hands across the silky fabric, I wondered if it would still fit me.

I hesitated, worried that I would look silly in a bright red dress at a wedding, even though it was a Valentine's Day wedding. Knowing I would see Martin again, my insides started to swirl. My nerves started to get the best of me, so I decided to pour out my anxious thoughts onto the blank pages of my trusty journal.

I am so nervous, I feel like I'm going to throw up. I am scared—I can admit that here, in these pages. What I can't seem to pinpoint is the reason why. I think I really blew it with Martin. He wanted to kiss me, but I wasn't ready for the change in our relationship status. I've come to really enjoy Martin's company and his steady presence. Now, I've lost even that. How do I come back from literally running away from him like that? Am I afraid of opening my heart, am I afraid of being alone forever, or am I afraid that I'm not good enough for someone as worldly as Martin, and I'm setting myself up for heartbreak?

After all, he's leaving for Mexico in a day or two, so if he was trying to kiss me, did he just want something casually physical from me? I am definitely not ready for something like that. If I open my heart, it will be for something real and permanent, not just a hook-up. I'm out of practice with navigating relationships—if I was even ever IN practice. After all, my only serious relationship was one I fell into with a friend when I was in high school and we drifted into marriage as the natural next step.

I've never "dated" a man before and I have no clue what I'm doing. I'm so apprehensive about seeing Martin today, but he has his duties as a member of the wedding party. I should be able to avoid him fairly easily, if he doesn't completely ignore me. What a mess! At least it will be over once he leaves for Mexico. I just have to hang on for a couple more days. While I can privately admit that I will miss Martin desperately, it will be better for my nerves when everything is back to the same old, same old.

I closed the journal and set it on my bedside table. I felt immensely better and my head was clearer. I squared my shoulders with new determination, picked up the hanger, stripped the dry cleaner's plastic bag off, dropped the robe, and slipped into the red dress.

I turned to look at my reflection in the mirrored closet door, and a stunning redhead with a tumble of curls and curves in all the right places looked back at me. The dress fit perfectly and magically hid any figure flaws while emphasizing all my best attributes. I barely recognized such a glamorous version of myself.

After touching up my makeup and adding some shimmering gold eyeshadow, black liquid eyeliner, and matte red lipstick, I decided to leave my hair down to tumble in a mass down my back. I slipped a large pair of simple hoops into my ears and strapped on some sparkly heeled sandals. After tucking my phone and a compact and my lipstick into a tiny gold evening bag, I grabbed my trusty wrap and headed out for the chapel.

*   *   *

I entered the doors of the Grace Chapel and I was immediately greeted by Mikki's father, Randall. He was a short but very animated man and he looked handsome in his suit.

"Hi, Lacey! How are you doing, gorgeous?" Randall enveloped me in a firm hug. I hugged him back, assured him that I was doing just fine.

"Bride's side?" Randall raised one bushy silver eyebrow theatrically.

"Yes, sir," I replied, taking his offered elbow as he ushered me to a seat halfway back on the left side of the chapel's pews.

There were red roses and baby's breath everywhere. The altar was set with sprays of roses and an unlit unity candle was waiting between two lit taper candles on either side. The chapel filled up quickly.

Randall escorted dozens of guests to their seats, including Mayor Reese and his daughter, Rayna. The two of them were seated towards the front of the chapel, directly behind the family row. The mayor was handsome, with his silver tipped temples and charcoal designer suit that fit him like a glove. Rayna was gorgeous as always with her waterfall of gleaming black hair and a silky couture gown in a gorgeous shade of violet that matched her eyes.

Soon, the chapel was filled with guests, the sound of their chatter echoing through the high-ceilinged room. The lights lowered and the soft background music changed to Pachelbel's Canon in D. The crowd settled into silence as the double doors at the back of the chapel opened. Mikki's mother, Ellen, swept in on the arm of Martin's older brother, Allan. The pair was followed by Mikki and Martin.

My heart lurched hard at the sight of Martin, in his pale gray suit and red tie. He had cut his hair, and it was now short enough that he no longer had the tumble of waves falling over his forehead. I thought he looked better with the longer hair, like an untamed male Brontë character, windswept and wild as the moors.

The attendants made their way to the altar and took their places on either side of Sheriff Weaver, who stood straight and proud in his dress uniform. The music faded out and the church choir stood and began to sing a gorgeous acapella version of the John Legend song "All of Me" as the rear doors opened again, and Joanna Morten appeared.

Her silver locks in elaborate braids winding around her head to create a coronet style looked magnificent topped with a sparkling filigree tiara. Her eyes glowed brightly and her cheeks flushed a flattering pink. She radiated pure joy as she moved up the aisle of the chapel.

The gown she wore was a creamy white silk with a lace overlay that was gently gathered just below the bust with sleeves that ended in a bell under the elbows. The lace neckline was high and accentuated the cameo pin that Jo wore at her throat. She carried a round bouquet of red roses, the tightly packed stems wrapped and tied in white ribbon. She floated down the aisle as if on a cloud.

Seeing how gorgeous and joyful Jo looked in her wedding gown, hearing the touching song, and thinking about Martin, I felt tears welling up in my eyes. I tried desperately not to cry. *There goes my meticulous makeup job.* I fumbled a tissue out of my bag and dabbed at my eyes carefully, trying to catch the tears before they fell.

Once Jo had made her way up the aisle and joined her misty-eyed groom, the song ended, and the couple made their vows and exchanged rings. The ceremony was short and sweet, and after the unity candle was lit the reverend invited

Sheriff Bob to kiss his bride. The choir stood again and began a robust version of "Walking on Sunshine" as the newly married couple kissed and the wedding party came back down the aisle.

As Martin passed my row, I made myself busy digging around in my tiny bag as if I were looking for something. I couldn't bring myself to look up and meet his eyes if he looked my way. I also couldn't bear the pain of seeing him *not* look my way, so I avoided the whole thing by pretending to ignore him.

I stood and filed out with the rest of the guests, and rushed through the receiving line, giving hugs to the bride and groom, and to Mikki and her mother. I shook Allan's hand, muttering something about how it was nice to see him, and then I found myself face to face with Martin.

"Martin," I said formally, holding out my hand. Martin took my hand in both of his and gave it a brief squeeze. His mouth turned up slightly at the corners but the tight smile didn't reach his eyes. The moment seemed to last forever, and yet it was over all too soon as the next guest crowded up behind me.

Martin released my hand. His eyes lingered on mine for a moment, but before I could read the expression within them, he turned his gaze to the next guest. I lurched along on legs that were numb and moving on instinct.

I had to get going, anyway. I needed to get to the ball and find Agnes so that she could provide me with the winner's name and a copy of their poem for the contest. I drove through the mess of traffic to park in the lot behind the old McKenna mansion. The massive building loomed against the twilight sky. Fairy lights twinkled over the pathway as I walked around to the front doors. I noticed Mayor Reese helping Rayna out of the backseat of a long black limousine. People with a bigger budget than I had were pulling up to the valet line and a parade of guests glittering in their formal best floated up the front walk.

I spotted Jed in a black suit, with Elaine on his arm. She wore a long and silky cream-colored sheath dress with cap sleeves and a red ribbon tied around the empire waist. The couple looked thrilled as they approached the ball.

As I walked through the doors, I followed the signs along the halls and stepped into the ballroom. My senses were overloaded with the music and the crowds of people and all the twinkling lights and metallic heart balloons. There was even a mirrored disco ball tossing bits of light around the shining hardwood floors.

Couples were dancing in the center of the room, and lots of people were gathered around the long tables lining the room that were laden with punch bowls and trays of hors d'oeuvres. On the table at the end of the room I saw a massive white wedding cake tastefully covered with red roses.

I heard a commotion at the main entrance to the room. The music faded and the DJ's voice boomed over the speakers, "I would like to announce the arrival of tonight's guests of honor. Please welcome Mr. and Mrs. Robert Weaver!" The crowd erupted into enthusiastic applause and whistling as a spotlight appeared and shone on the couple in the doorway. Jo and Bob waved, and Jo blew kisses into the crowd.

"Thank goodness, I've been looking everywhere for you," a voice hissed at my elbow. I turned to find Agnes, in a red crepe pantsuit, clutching three envelopes that she thrust at me. I took them and saw that they were all sealed.

"Thanks, Agnes. You look nice," I said.

"Thanks, and you look absolutely gorgeous," she replied with a wink.

"So which envelope is which?" I asked.

"Red one is the winner, pink one has the copy of the poem in it for you to read aloud, and the white one has the Visa gift card in it," she said, patting my forearm. "The mayor wants to do the poetry contest announcement right after he makes his welcome speech, then after you make the announcement and do the reading, the bride and groom will cut the wedding cake." She rubbed her hands together. "And then, we can really party!"

I laughed and waved her off, telling her to go get some punch, and looked around for the mayor. I spotted him talking to the DJ and figured that he was discussing the timing of his speech. Sure enough, as soon as the song ended, the DJ leaned over his microphone.

"Hello, good folks of Pinewood Corners, and welcome to this year's annual Cupid's Ball. As we get started tonight, we'll kick things off with an announcement. Please welcome Mayor Reese!"

Mayor Reese took the podium to a scattering of applause and the spotlight reappeared. The distinguished man adjusted his tie and cleared his throat. Feedback squealed over the speakers as he started to speak into the microphone. The crowd reacted by covering their ears and frowning as the noise settled.

"Sorry, everyone. As I was trying to say, I would like to congratulate Bob and Joanna Weaver on their wedding, and thank them for celebrating with us at the Cupid's Ball tonight." He paused for the round of cheers.

"I would also like to extend my gratitude to Lacey Crawford and Martin Weaver for their efforts to bring to light a important piece of the history of Pinewood Corners when they were able to locate not only precious journals and letters from the wife of our town's founder, but also discover the truth of her story." He flashed a toothy white grin. "Not to mention finding the priceless legendary Valentine's necklace!"

The crowd erupted in cheers and to my dismay, a spotlight appeared on me. I didn't know if one appeared on Martin, I hadn't seen him arrive, and I was blinded by the brightness of the light aimed at me.

"Furthermore," Mayor Reese announced, "we've found the rightful owner of the necklace through the family trees and various records, and we've confirmed our information through DNA kit databases." A hush came over the crowd. The mayor, as a politician, knew how to work the crowd and draw out the drama. "The last living descendant of the McKenna family is none other than our very own favorite pet lover, Colleen Perkins! Colleen, why don't you come up here and say a few words?"

The spotlight was on Colleen now who stood in a daze, blinking and smiling. She made her way to the podium. Her dress was candy pink and she had on an actual pink feather boa. I grinned at the ensemble.

"Thank you, Mayor Reese," she said, leaning too close to the mic and blurring her consonants. "I was so shocked and I couldn't have been more surprised when you all informed me that I was a direct descendant of the daughter of Maeve McKenna, the daughter that nobody knew existed until Martin and Lacey uncovered the truth. I mean, I just could not have been more amazed than if I had won the lottery, which I kind of did, if you think about it, because—" she stopped for a moment as the mayor gave her a stern look.

"Anyway," she continued, "I wanted to announce that I'm going to allow the necklace to be on display in the Pinewood Corners History Museum, and I'm going to purchase the old Riley place and turn it into a pet-friendly bed-and-breakfast establishment!" The crowd exploded into cheers and applause once more and Colleen beamed.

"Thank you, Colleen, for your generosity," Mayor Reese said, dismissing the blonde gracefully. "And now we have a special treat to get you all in a romantic mood for tonight's ball." Mayor Reese beckoned to me. "The Pinewood Corners Public Library has sponsored a love poetry contest on their website. The winning entry was voted on by the library patrons, and the winning poet receives a fifty dollar Visa gift card."

There were a couple of whoops and cheers, and the mayor went on. "And here to announce the winner and read the poem is our favorite head librarian, Lacey Crawford." He gestured to me as I stepped up to the podium, clinging to the envelopes with my sweaty hands.

I waited for the applause to die down before I spoke.

"Thank you to everyone who entered the contest, and who voted. Thank you to all of our loyal patrons as well, because we wouldn't have a library if it wasn't for all of you. And now, without further ado, the winner of the first annual Sweetheart Soiree love poetry contest is …"

I placed the envelopes on the surface of the podium. I remembered that pink contained the poem because they both started with a "P" and the white envelope contained the gift card, so I picked up the red envelope and tore it open.

"The winning poet is—it's um—" my throat dried up suddenly and I gulped. "It's Martin Weaver."

Mayor Reese was smiling and the crowd clapped and cheered. I fumbled for the pink envelope and with trembling fingers, I removed the folded white paper. I smoothed it out and the words there swam in front of my eyes. The mayor kept smiling and nodded encouragingly at me to go on.

I took a deep breath and slowly released it, gripping the sides of the podium with white knuckles as I began to read the lines of the poem aloud.

"Red Gold," by Martin Weaver

In a world awash with shades, a radiant ringlet
unfurls,
A tapestry of love, adorned with red-gold curls.
She walks with intellect, a beacon shining bright,
Smart and witty, she weaves her laughter
And vivid sunrise colors into my gray life.

Her mind, a kaleidoscope of thoughts, a dazzling
spree,
A symphony of brilliance, a wonder to see.
In the gallery of uniqueness, she's a vibrant display,
A living canvas of colors, in her own charming way.
Her laughter, a melody that dances on the air,
A serenade of joy, beyond compare.

Funny and quick-witted, a sparkling repartee,
Singing off-key with Taylor and Stevie.
Her humor, a treasure, a source of jubilee.
In a world of monotony, she stands as a muse,
A vision of boldness, where individuality infuses.
Her style, a palette of random hues, a fashion fright
or delight,
A masterpiece of uniqueness, a true delight.

Red-gold curls, like sunbeams in a golden dawn,
A crown of warmth, a beauty to fawn.

In her gaze, intelligence sparkles, a celestial glow,
A constellation of wisdom, in her eyes aglow.
She's a symphony of colors in a world of black and
white,
A mosaic of laughter, a brilliant light.

In the canvas of existence, she's a stroke so fine,
A masterpiece of love, forever entwined.
My love belongs to the woman with red-gold tresses
so rare,
Smart, funny, and colorful, beyond compare.
In my lonely heart so dark and cold she shines.
In the gallery of hearts, where emotions run wild,
She's a masterpiece of love, forever I'm beguiled.

As I finished reading, my voice broke and a hush of reverence permeated the room for a moment. Then the crowd exploded with an enthusiastic roar of applause.

Colleen, still standing nearby, leaned in and said, "Wow, I think that poem might be about you!"

I just stood there, feeling so overwhelmed with swirling emotions that I was practically paralyzed and felt as if my spirit had left my body and I was watching things unfold from far away. Mayor Reese asked me if I was going to present the gift card, and I came crashing back to earth with a bang.

"Oh, yes, of course." I snatched up the white envelope. "Mr. Weaver, if you'll please come up and accept your prize." I waved the envelope in the air. The crowds parted, and there he was. Martin made his way past the throngs of people and up to the podium. As he wove towards me, his burning amber eyes never left my face.

He stepped up to the podium next to me and plucked the envelope from my fingers. *He still smells so good, like wood and whiskey and leather and home.*

"Thank you, everyone, for reading my poem and voting for it. It means a lot to me, because it was written for someone very special." He looked into my eyes, more deeply than anyone ever had before, and I felt completely seen and accepted for the first time. He reached up and brushed a lock of hair away from my face and cupped my chin.

He whispered to me so that only I could hear, "Are you ready now, Lacey? Is this okay?"

I nodded, not trusting myself to speak, as his lips met mine in a soul-melting kiss that fried all my circuits to the point where I completely forgot where I was. I kissed him back with gusto, reaching up to run my hands through his hair. I definitely had to ask him to grow it back out. Gradually, I realized that the partygoers were now whooping and wolf-whistling. I broke away and a flush of heat colored my cheeks, so bright it rivaled my red dress.

"Let's go talk, somewhere out of the public eye," Martin whispered.

"Yes," I said and squeezed his forearm. "Thank you, everyone," I said loudly into the microphone as we left the podium together to more applause. I heard the mayor telling everyone to have a fun and safe evening as the music started back up again.

Martin kept his hand at the small of my back as we exited the ballroom and followed a corridor to a small alcove with a bench. We collapsed together side by side on the bench and immediately began talking over each other.

"I missed you so much," we both said and then our laughter mixed together. Martin kissed me again, more slowly this time. He smiled but his expression was heated with passion.

"I've been wanting to do that since I first saw you waddling around your car that morning in the library's parking lot," he said fondly.

"Really? I wanted to stab you with my keys because I thought you were an intruder," I said through my laughter.

"Well I'm glad you didn't."

"Great job, winning the poetry contest. I thought you didn't like emotional lyrics?"

"I didn't," Martin caressed my cheek. "Not until I actually understood the sentiments."

"Martin?" I looked away. "What's next? You have to leave for Mexico now, and I have a life here, with Claire and the library. Pinewood Corners is my home. I can't leave."

Martin stroked my head gently. "I love your hair, Lacey. I dream about these red-gold curls."

I turned back to look at him once again. "I'm flattered, but that doesn't answer my question. I thought I would go crazy being apart from you for a week. How can I bear you being away in Mexico and who knows where else after that? What if—what if you don't come back?" My voice was small and unsure.

Martin continued to toy with my ringlets. "I can't get out of the dig in Mexico, but I can assure you that I have plenty of experience with the area and the people there. I'll be gone for a few months, but after that …" he trailed off, apparently fascinated by my hair.

"Martin," I said impatiently, grasping his wrist.

"After that, I heard there's a position open for a new world history teacher at Pinewood High School this fall."

"Really? You're thinking about giving up your vagabond Indiana Jones lifestyle? I don't want you to change your life for me, and end up resenting me down the line."

"It's a lonely life, to tell you the truth, but it didn't bother me so much when I didn't know what it meant to want to settle down with someone." He looked into my eyes again. "Before I knew what it was like to be in love with someone."

I looked down at my lap, plucking at my dress nervously. "Love?"

He placed a finger under my chin and gently lifted my head to look into my eyes. "Lacey, I love you, all of you, exactly as you are. I love your wildly mismatched and unique style, I love how you are with Claire. I even love your off-key singing with Stevie Nicks."

We kissed again, and my inner walls, constructed so long ago around my heart, burst completely. I felt them shatter and wash away in the flood of love that flowed out from the center of my chest. I had never felt so vulnerable and so safe at the same time. I knew that I could trust this man with my heart and my love. I sighed gently as we pulled away from the kiss.

"Well, I guess we could give it a try. Eastern Mexico is only one hour behind, in the Central time zone. We can keep in touch over FaceTime, texts, calls, and emails. And maybe in the fall … "

"I could find an apartment and start that new teaching job," Martin chimed in. "My dad's getting older, and I know he would appreciate having one of his kids close by."

"And you know, it would be wonderful to celebrate all the holidays together, what with Jo being an honorary grandma to Claire already, and now she's married to your dad—"

"He would be a fantastic grandpa to Claire."

I sobered after a moment. "I guess we'll never know what really happened to JP after Maeve staged her disappearance."

"It's not likely, but it does appear that once Maeve vanished, JP did as well, so it seems that she was successful in escaping him."

"Where do you think she went in the year she was gone, when she gave birth to Colleen, before she showed up on the Hanrahan's doorstep in disguise, looking for work as a maid?"

"We'll probably never know the truth about that, either." Martin leaned close and inhaled the scent of my hair.

"I hope she ended up happy."

"Me, too. At least she was free."

I sighed and leaned my head against Martin's shoulder, taking in his scent and his warmth and the grounding feel of his energy. He held my hand and traced circles on my palm with his thumb.

"By the way, the 'P' in Martin P. Weaver? It stands for Phineas. Don't tell anyone."

Laughing, I slid my arms around his waist and held on tightly as I whispered, "Your secret is safe with me. And I love you, too, Martin."

Three Months Later

"**M**iriam, I'm taking my lunch break now," I called out as I jogged towards my office. It was just about 12:30. Miriam shot me a knowing smile and waved me along. I made it into my office and had just shut the door when I heard my cell chime.

I grabbed the phone off the desk and eagerly hit the green button to accept the FaceTime call. Martin's face appeared on the screen.

"Hi, honey!" I cried,

"Hey, babe, you look beautiful! How's your day going?" Martin grinned and tossed his head, flipping his wavy mop of hair. He had let it grow out again at my request. I sighed over him mentally for a moment before replying.

"My day is good, but busy. I barely got away in time for our call. Between construction on the new library wing, and putting all the new programs in place, it's been crazy around here. Crazy but wonderful! I mean, the grant that Janine's foundation provided to the library was so generous. I don't know how I can ever thank her."

"Just make sure you spell her name right on the commemorative plaque," Martin suggested dryly. "The dig is going well, but I miss you, and I miss Claire. I can't wait to see you guys next month when I'm off for two weeks." His smile reflected brilliantly in his eyes.

"I know, I'm counting the days," I held up my day planner from my desk to show all the hearts with descending numbers written in them on each day, counting down to the day Martin would arrive back in Pinewood Corners. "See, literally counting them down." I put the calendar back on the desk.

"Plus," I said, "there's lots of excitement over Colleen's new bed-and-breakfast. She's received a lot of publicity, because of her family heritage and the necklace and everything. The mayor is thrilled that the necklace on display has increased visitors to the town. He's expecting record-breaking attendance at the Harvest Happenings festival this fall. I guess Colleen's establishment will be opening just in time!"

"And the pet-friendly aspect will be good for business as well," Martin agreed.

"Oh, she's already got people asking when they can make a reservation." I glanced up at the clock on my office wall. "Ready for lunch?" I asked. I held up a grease-stained bag with the Logan's Lunch logo on it, and a cup of lemonade as I wiggled my eyebrows provocatively.

Martin groaned. "Woman, what are you trying to do to me? You know how much I love Logan's sandwiches!"

"Well, I guess I want to make sure that you *really* want to come home as soon as possible," I laughed.

Martin held up a wrapped sandwich. "Not as delicious as your lunch, but it will do." We unwrapped our sandwiches and dug in together.

"I love you, Lacey," Martin said thickly through a mouthful.

I gave a thumbs up and swallowed before replying, "I love you, too, Martin."

As I enjoyed my favorite meatball sub, I reflected on how much better it tasted when enjoyed in the company of a kindred spirit. We chatted about anything and everything, while the sounds of the bustling library went on outside my office door.

My life had seemed full before, but now it was bursting with promise. My career was blossoming, the library was growing by leaps and bounds, Claire would be starting kindergarten next year, and I was overjoyed to be getting to know Martin on a deeper level.

The afternoon sunlight filtered in through the window, lighting up the room with a golden glow that filled my heart with joy. For the first time in a very long while, I was completely content with who I was and with where my life was headed, and I was looking forward to what the future would bring.

The End

Stay tuned for the next book in the Pinewood Corners series, *The Harvest Moon's Hope* to find out how Colleen's bed-and-breakfast fares. Will she find success and romance as a business owner and a newly minted heiress? Coming Fall 2024.

About the Author

Carol Babineaux has always loved stories about love. She is from the southwest desert, and her fond childhood memories of celebrating holidays surrounded by treasured family, delicious food, and great music inspired her to pen the Pinewood Corners Sweet Romance series. Carol has enjoyed a long career in administration and has a diploma in Integrative Healing and Hypnotherapy from the Southwest Institute of Healing Arts. When she isn't writing, she can be found in yoga class, reading, cooking, watching movies, and spending time with family and friends. Carol lives in Arizona with her husband and a gaggle of cats.

carolbabineaux.com

The Pinewood Corners Sweet Romance Series

The Christmas Cookie Conundrum (Nov. 2023)

The St. Valentine's Situation (Feb. 2024)

The Harvest Moon's Hope (Fall 2024)

Follow Carol on Amazon:

bit.ly/carolbabineaux

9 7 9 8 9 8 9 6 5 4 8 8 8

The Stars
We
Never
Saw

EMILIE GARRABRANT

ISBN: 979-8-9866757-0-1 paperback
ISBN: 979-8-9866757-2-5 e-book